Get Wreckt

B.E.N.T.
Biological Enhanced Nascent Talent

By Kal Spriggs

Three Ravens Publishing
Chickamauga, GA USA

GET WRECKT By Kal Spriggs
Published by Three Ravens Publishing
threeravenspublishing@gmail.com
P O Box 851, Chickamauga, Ga 30707
https://www.threeravenspublishing.com
Copyright © 2025 by Kal Spriggs

Publishers Note: This is a work of fiction. Names, characters, places, and incidents are a product of the author's imagination. Locales and public names are sometimes used for atmospheric purposes. Any resemblance to actual people, living or dead, or to businesses, companies, events, institutions, or locales is completely coincidental.

Credits:
GET WRECKT was written by Kal Spriggs

Cover Design by: J.F. Posthumus

Mass Market Paperback ISBN: 978-1-966507-31-4
Ebook ISBN: 978-1-966507-30-7

Contents

Chapter 1 1

Chapter 2 13

Chapter 3 23

Chapter 4 33

Chapter 5 51

Chapter 6 69

Chapter 7 85

Chapter 8 99

Chapter 9 121

Chapter 10 139

Chapter 11 157

Chapter 12 171

Chapter 13 191

Chapter 14 213

Chapter 15 227

Chapter 16 243

Chapter 17 249

Chapter 1

“Do it, do it now, do it harder!” Arnold Wreckt shouted. His impressive muscles strained beneath his skin, sweat glistening across his entire body.

“Yeah, harder!” The two workout girls on either side cheered.

“Alright, we’re going to knock out ten minutes of the hardest workout you’ve ever done, and say it with me: You’ll get Wreckt!” Wreckt called out, his harsh voice terrifyingly enthusiastic.

Alright, this is going good… We needed enthusiastic, we needed this to go well. Arnold wasn’t what he used to be, and right now, his fitness show, *Get Wreckt*, was all that was keeping us afloat. Thirty years ago, he had been doing action movies. Now the best we could do was this.

Arnold smiled at the camera. “Now remember, boys and girls—”

“Cut, cut!” Frankie shouted. “What the hell, Wreckt? We went over this!” The director hurried up, his pale-yellow leisure suit stained with sweat from the combined Chicago summer heat and all the production lights.

The two fitness girls looked pissed, and one got out her pack of cigarettes.

"What?" Wreckt looked over in surprise.

I got out of my chair and headed over, even as Frankie went into it, "You can't say 'boys and girls' anymore, Wreckt. We're trying to be gender-neutral, right, Tammy?"

Tammy blew a puff of cigarette smoke. "Yeah, sure, whatever."

"Right." Frankie nodded at Wreckt.

"Look, Frankie, I'm sorry," I said as I came up next to Wreckt. "We'll run it again and—"

"No, no, I'm done reminding your client, Eddie." Frankie turned on me. "I'm done with the both of you. Chappo, get over here!"

"Boss?" Chappo came over. He was a big black man, muscled like Wreckt had been in his heyday, maybe even more so. I wasn't going to say that Chappo did a lot of 'roids, but I would bet his sperm count was lower than his IQ.

"We're recasting you, Wreckt. Chappo, get in there," Frankie told him.

"You can't recast me, this is my show, I am the fitness star!" Wreckt complained. He had a point, and I was scratching my head as to exactly what was going on.

"Your tits are saggier than my ex-wife's, and I've seen more enthusiasm from my dead mother," Frankie scoffed. "You haven't done a strongman competition in twenty years, you haven't placed in one in thirty years. You're killing us on the lonely housewives demographic. Chappo, strip down to the costume. Show them the costume."

Chappo pulled off his jogging suit, stripping down to not much more than a speedo.

"He doesn't look anything like Arnold," I told Frankie.

"We've got enough footage to run a deepfake on his face and voice," Frankie scoffed at me. "Your client signed away all digital rights to his appearance in the contract."

I winced at that. I remembered reading that part and thinking it meant spin-off video games or something like that. I would never have imagined they'd digitize a complete replacement for him.

"But… he's black," Wreckt protested.

"We'll fix it in post-production, auf-wider-sain, Wreckt, get lost." Frankie turned away.

I hurried around and blocked his path. "We have a contract, Frankie, this show, it has my client's name—"

"Thank you, Eddie, for that reminder. I already had the lawyers draft this up." Frankie reached inside his leisure suit jacket and pulled out a folded document. "Here is a cease and desist letter for you and your 'client.' Get Wreckt Productions owns all rights to the Wreckt Brand. That includes catchphrases, slogans, and most importantly, names. Wreckt is owned by Get Wreckt Productions. Your client needs to stop using our name since he no longer represents Get Wreckt Productions."

"That's his legal name, jackass." I lost my temper.

"Not anymore." Frankie waved a hand at Wreckt and then me. "Arnold, you and your flying monkey go ahead and get off my set, or I'll have you removed."

"You and what army?" Wreckt asked in an ominous tone. He did that well, especially when he was angry.

"Chappo!" Frankie called.

Chappo came over. "Yeah, boss?"

"Please escort *Arnold* and his little pet here off the premises." Frankie sneered.

Wreckt stepped forward, but I'd sized up Chappo, and more importantly, the slavering lawyer who seemed to appear at Frankie's side, and Arnold Wreckt wasn't at his prime anymore. Best case, he beat Chappo's ass and then Frankie's lawyer sued us into oblivion. Worst case, Chappo beat Wreckt and me and *still* sued us into oblivion.

I got between my client and the director. "Arnold, let's go, screw these guys, we don't need them."

For a moment, he pushed against me, making my feet skid on the concrete floor. Then, as if with great reluctance, he turned away. I fell in next to him, knowing he was still pretty volatile. I chattered at him as we walked out, "Yeah, we don't need these losers anyway. There's loads of places that we can work…"

I kept it up until we got out of the warehouse.

"Sorry, Eddie," Wreckt told me as we got outside. "I thought it was going so well."

That makes one of us. I kept that thought to myself. I was Wreckt's only friend, sure, but he was also my meal ticket. Neither one of us had done well in Hollywood, not in decades, anyway. As much as I didn't want to say it, I hadn't done him any great works as his agent, either.

It didn't help that I looked like a sixteen-year-old. That was *my* problem, really, I was forty-five years old, and I looked and sounded like a teenage boy. Even aside from how Arnold Wreckt and I had pissed various people off over the years, it made getting taken seriously as Wreckt's agent a little hard.

"It's not your fault, show business, what'cha gonna do?" I told him. I pulled out a cigarette and lit up.

"Those things are bad for you." Arnold shook his head.

"Yeah, lots of things are bad for me…" I looked around, wondering what we should do next. Wreckt was standing there, still in his fitness gear. He looked ridiculous, not that I'd tell him that.

"You shouldn't let your son smoke," an older woman snapped at him as she walked past us.

"You should go fuck yourself, lady, I'm old enough to vote!" I called after her. I was BENT, Biologically Enhanced Nascent Talent. It wasn't my fault I looked sixteen, some weird alien shit had messed with my genes and made me this way.

That drew stares from passersby, and in this part of Chicago, that probably wasn't a good thing. Frankie paid off the local gangbangers for protection of the filming site. Unfortunately, we weren't covered anymore, and I would bet that Frankie was a spiteful enough guy to let them know that.

If some bum shanked Wreckt, then we'd really be screwed.

"Let's go." I patted Arnold on the shoulder. We started down the street. Chicago was really going downhill, but Frankie had set it up here because the production company could buy a whole swath of buildings on the cheap to film from.

Every building on the street had plywood where the windows had been. The whole block had an air of abandonment and despair. It looked worse than post-apocalyptic movie sets I had been on. For all that, it still looked better than parts of Los Angeles.

"So, as soon as we get back to our place, I'll start making some calls," I told Wreckt as we walked. I kept my head on a swivel, eyeing for threats to either of us. Not that I knew what to do about them, other than hustling Wreckt in the other direction.

"Do you think that will help?" he asked, his harsh voice doubtful. "You told me that this was our last option."

I winced as he remembered what I had told him when we started this project. "I know I said that, but this is show business, new things always pop up, look—"

I broke off as we heard a scream and the sound of flesh striking flesh. We both spun around, him just a fraction of a second ahead of me.

Down the alley, almost at the far end, a man had just hit a woman. "Wreckt…" I started to say.

"You, asshole, stop right there," Wreckt shouted, his voice far louder in the street than I would like.

Before I could stop him, he took off at a run down the alley. He was big, and he wasn't as spry as he used to be, but at over six feet, and he did a lot of cardio, he took off faster than someone his size had any business moving.

"Shit, shit, shit," I cursed under my breath and ran after him.

Wreckt didn't bother with jumping trash cans or running around puddles, he plowed through everything in his path, knocking shit everywhere as I ran behind him, shouting, "Stop, wait, stop, shit!"

I wasn't exactly slow myself, a benefit of having the body of a teenager, I suppose, and I had almost caught up to him when we ran through a cloud of dust or steam or something.

I had been taking big whooping breaths, trying to catch up to Wreckt, when I ran through it, and whatever it was, it was in my eyes, my lungs, and my brain. It burned, it burned like nothing had burned since I had been sixteen and I had done some really stupid shit.

I burst out of the cloud of dust right behind Wreckt, only I wasn't right behind him for long. It was like he had turned on the afterburners, and he took off like a jet. He was moving so fast I saw trash cans being pulled into the alleyway in his wake.

He closed the last hundred feet or so between him and the woman's attacker faster than I could shout any further warnings. One arm out, he hit the thug, and then there was a wet-sounding thud as the perp spun end over end and splatted against the side of a garbage truck across the street.

The remains of the woman's attacker slowly dribbled down the side of the truck, and there were people coming up to look.

"Aw shit, aw shit." I hurried forward.

Wreckt had helped the woman to her feet. In true Chicago fashion, she slapped him. "Get the hell off me, white boy!"

I caught Wreckt by the elbow, and I led him away. "Dammit, man, what the hell was that?" I muttered at him as I started getting him out of there. The last thing we needed was a murder charge.

A glance back over my shoulder showed a crowd gathering around the fallen mugger. No one was pointing or looking in our direction, not yet, anyway. Hopefully they would write it off as a hit and run, with a car or something. A really big heavy German car that didn't know to mind its own business.

"I don't know, I just lost it when I saw him hitting her," Wreckt told me.

"Arnold, we've been over this, we can't just get involved." I didn't look at him as we hurried down the street. I got us to the bus stop and on the bus and seated. We were still drawing more attention than I wanted, and I glanced at Wreckt.

I had to do a double take. Arnold looked like he had gotten a total body makeover. He looked like he had when he was in his twenties. Better than he had in his twenties. He looked like he had just stepped out of his first place win of Mister Universe—before they started letting Talents in, and they won it and every strongman competition ever since.

"Holy shit, Wreckt, what happened to you?" I demanded.

"What do you mean?" He looked down at himself. "I feel fine, I feel better than fine. Is something wrong?"

"I mean…" I shook my head. "You look like you just got a total body makeover. Like *really* good plastic surgery." I stared at him. "You… you look like a Talent."

He raised one hand and stared at it and then clenched it into a fist. "I feel strong."

I had no idea what had happened. I had always thought Arnold Wreckt was a BENT, at least a little bit. He always was too strong and too big. Even so, he had also worked out every day, so it had been hard to tell.

Now, though, he looked as if he had the full works. His muscles had muscles. He had more definition than the dictionary. I poked him, just to see if it was real, and I bruised my finger. "Holy crap, man, we can make a lot of money off this."

Wreckt shook his head. "What do you mean?"

"Look, you look better than ever. We can slap you in a movie, we got the awesome eye candy again," I told him. "You look fantastic again, Arnold."

"I have been fantastic," he protested. "I work out three times a day, I put in the time."

"Arnold…" I shook my head. "I mean, you kind of had the dad bod, only with extra muscles strapped on. Now, though, now we can get you cast again, this is great news, buddy." I had no idea how it had happened. Maybe he had been struck by lightning or something, maybe it had just taken the jolt of adrenaline when he had rushed to save the woman. Maybe it had been that weird smoke we had run through in the alleyway. I didn't know or care.

Wreckt didn't seem particularly impressed. That was fine, I'd handle the business, he just had to do his thing and look good. "As soon as we get back to the apartment, I'll make some calls."

Chapter 2

"Tony, yeah, hey, how you doing?" I smiled as I talked into my cell phone, already settling into the pitch.

Behind me, Wreckt was lifting weights. I could see him putting more weights on the bars, testing them, then adding more. True to form, he also had a book out, and he would set it down while he read, pausing in his weights to turn a page before going back to it.

"Yeah, this is Eddie… no, not Eddie Van Halen, he's been dead several years." I gritted my teeth as I spoke. Tony had never been a bright one. "Eddie *Connor*, remember… hello? Tony?"

I looked down at the phone. "He hung up on me."

"Hah, look at this," Arnold said from behind me. I turned around to see him lifting two different deadlift bars, each one full of weights, one with each arm. There was plenty of room in our loft apartment for it. Besides his weights, we didn't have any other furniture, really, an oversized mattress for Wreckt, an air mattress for me, a couple of cheap folding chairs, and a table missing a leg. The production studio had paid for the apartment, which meant we probably needed to find a new place to stay. I was half surprised they didn't have someone here to change the locks already.

"Nice, don't hurt yourself, and don't break the floor," I told him. I pulled up another number on my phone and took a deep breath.

"Hello, Kathleen, hey, yeah, it's Eddie, how are you doing?" I waited and then nodded and smiled, even though she couldn't see me. "Yeah, that's great. I loved what you did with the franchise, really great, I can't believe it didn't break the box office. Yeah, some people really don't know what culture and art is, I agree, especially when you showed the world what a strong female character really is, yeah."

I paused as she began a rant, and I waited her out. "Yeah, that's really true. So, anyway, I was wondering if you have any spots in your next episode in the franchise. No, not for me, I appreciate that, but for Wreckt…"

She started laughing on the other end. "Yeah, um, I'm serious, he's looking really good, and…"

She brayed laughter loud enough that I had to pull the phone away from my ear. I felt my face growing hot as she laughed at me and my friend.

This time I pulled the phone back and yelled at it, "Yeah, well you ruined the only bright spot in my childhood with your stupid cow! You couldn't produce a movie if your life depended on it!"

She hung up on me, still braying with laughter.

I heard a clang and spun around. Wreckt was juggling barbells, laughing while he did it. "Look at this, Eddie, can you believe it?"

I pinched the bridge of my nose. "That's awesome, man, just don't damage the place, and don't hurt yourself, right?"

I was six for six on strikeouts. I only had one other number to try. I dialed it, my fingers shaking a bit. "Harvey? Hey, yeah, it's Eddie. No, not that Eddie. The other one, Eddie Connor. Uh huh. Yeah."

He said something rather rude, but I kept my cool. "I know last time we ran into each other, I may have said some things, and you may have said some things, and we both regret what was said…"

He said something else rather rude. "Alright, maybe I was a little out of line. Anyway, I'm not calling about me, Harvey, I'm calling about my client."

He said something rather unpleasant about me.

"My *client*," I repeated. "Remember Arnold Wreckt? He's looking really good, I think he'd be a great shoe-in for your next movie."

On the other end, Harvey said something rude.

I forced myself to be friendly and calm. "Yeah, well, that's probably an old picture. He's looking great, better than ever. That fitness thing, it was just testing the water, yeah. I don't care what Frankie told you, he's looking fantastic, he could bench press a cement truck right now."

At that point, he called me a liar and said some further rude things about me.

"Look, if you don't believe me, just schedule us in for a casting. I promise, he'll knock your socks off. Doesn't matter what part, what role, he's good for it…"

He cut me off. I listened for a minute, my face flushing red as he went on.

"Okay, I get it, Harvey, you want an apology. You want me to apologize. I can do that," I told him.

He went on a bit in my ear again.

"You want to hear me apologize, right now?" I asked. "Like, here, on the phone?"

He waited.

I took a deep breath. The words didn't seem to come at first. I told myself this was about business. An apology like this didn't mean a thing, it was all pretend. All I had to do was make the scumbag think I was sorry. This was acting, nothing more. I had been an actor, a good one. Now, I just had to act a little bit to get Wreckt a job.

"Harvey, I am sorry for what happened." I was proud of how level I kept my voice.

He said something then, and it was all I could do not to scream.

"You want me to apologize for what Wreckt did?" I asked incredulously.

The words came before I could help myself. "Harvey, I am sorry he broke your jaw. I'm sorry he didn't shatter your skull and kill you, you slimy, child molesting, worthless piece of crap…"

He hung up on me.

"I probably could have handled that one better," I muttered at the phone.

I spun at a crash and thud behind me, followed by a loud clang, multiple crashes, and the shattering of glass. Arnold had misjudged his own strength, and one barbell had gone up through the ceiling of our loft apartment. It hung half through the roof, debris raining down. Arnold had missed catching the other, and it had slammed through the floor and downstairs into the next apartment. I could hear shouts down there already.

I put my hands over my face. "Arnold, *really*, man?"

"I missed." He shrugged. He reached up and caught the one in the ceiling and pulled it down, ripping down a big chunk of ceiling with it. A couple of pieces of concrete bounced off his shoulders and skull, not that he noticed.

"Alright, crap, someone's going to call the cops on us now." I shook my head. We probably couldn't stay here anyway, Get Wreckt Productions had paid for the apartment, and Frankie had almost certainly canceled our lease. *I don't think you're getting back your deposit, Frankie.*

"Pack your stuff, just what you really need," I told him.

"Where are we going?" Wreckt asked. Other than his weights, I knew he had less than I did.

"I have one last lead. Remember that producer here in Chicago, the one who did the *Bullets, Blades, and Babes* movies?" I looked up as I asked.

"Oh, yeah, they were really good, especially the one with the cyborg who fired machine guns out of her knockers." Arnold nodded.

"Yeah, that guy, Norm Linus, I got his home address from a friend. He lives here in Chicago. He is about as burned by Hollywood as we are, but maybe we can get a movie going," I told him. I didn't have much hope for that. Arnold Wreckt and I were blacklisted because neither of us could keep our mouths shut in the face of awful people like Harvey Moore.

The guy we were going to see, he was the other way, he had a reputation for political ideas that the rest of the big names in Hollywood hated. I didn't care about the politics, I just wanted to have a roof over my head and for Wreckt to get the fame and fortune he deserved.

"Should we be doing a movie?" Wreckt asked. "I mean, most people, when they have a Talent, they do the hero or villain thing, right?"

I didn't know if what he had *was* a Talent. I mean, he was strong, maybe stronger than he had been at the height of his weight lifting and strongman days. I thought people were born with Talents, though, we all just had what we had. As far as I knew, the only time anyone *gained* Talents was when the meteor came over seventy years earlier.

"That's because they're shortsighted, Arnold." I continued to stuff things into my roller suitcase. The advantage of living on the ragged edge was that I didn't have a lot of possessions to pack. I just had a few changes of clothes, really, and Wreckt had even less. "Who wants to be a hero? That just comes with a bunch of insurance bills and puts a target on your back. And neither of us are cut out for the villain thing." I pointed at myself. "This face is way too pretty for prison."

"I think I killed that guy I hit earlier," Wreckt pointed out.

I looked up. "Nah, he probably walked it off, forget about it." I stuffed the last of my clothes and a few meager possessions into the roller case. I paused as I grabbed a picture. It was of Wreckt and I on the set of the last major movie either of us had starred in: *Roboslayer Three*. I looked almost the same, and Wreckt… I looked over at him, and he looked like he had then.

I threw the picture in the case. I had none of my parents or anyone else. For good reason, too. No one but Arnold Wreckt had ever helped me. No one had lifted a finger when my life had self-destructed. For thirty years, now, there had been the two of us, scraping by, getting what gigs I could for him.

That movie was where we had met. It was where he had broken Harvey Moore's jaw, too, which put a pause on the movie production, eventually killed the movie, and got both of us fired. Everything that had happened there had led, eventually, to where we were now.

There have been a few other major events, of course. For just a moment, I thought about the fire, and I shuddered. That was in the past, I had come back from that. I had determined to hell with Hollywood, I would make my own way.

In a way, I was kind of glad that none of the seven people I'd called had been willing to see Wreckt. In many ways, it would have been admitting defeat, going back to them, taking their table scraps and being their dog again.

Better we make our own way, I told myself.

"Let's go, man," I told Wreckt.

Get Wreckt

Chapter 3

"Should we be doing this?" Arnold asked as we slunk through the bushes in the twilight of evening. It had taken us most of the afternoon on various bus rides to get here, and we were quickly losing daylight.

"Yeah, this is fine, actors do this thing all the time to meet directors," I assured him as we got up to the back of the house. We had left the roller bags in the bushes near the wall, which Wreckt and I had climbed over. It was a nice house, not huge, but with a wall around the backyard, and it was clearly well-maintained.

Our producer lived in northern Chicago, in nicer areas than our crappy apartment. I had tried knocking on the front door, and he hadn't answered. Now, we were trying to be more proactive about finding him. I knew if I got my chance to make a pitch in person, I would get him to listen to me, especially once he saw Wreckt.

"Here we are," I said in a low voice as we reached the back door. "Open it."

"I don't have a key," Wreckt protested.

"Get the handle and pull real hard," I told him.

He did that and pulled the handle right off the door.

I bit back a curse and went around to the window. It wasn't locked, and I slid it up. The inside was dark, and I climbed through carefully, moving as quiet as I could, until I got to the back door. I had to fiddle with it in the dark before I finally got it open.

Wreckt slipped inside, knocking over a small table with a loud clatter in the process, and I flinched at the noise.

"Alright, now we just find him and—"

"Who the hell are you?" a voice asked as the lights came up.

I blinked in the bright light. Then, I blinked in shock. A middle-aged man was taped to an office chair, his eyes wide, with a section of tape over his mouth. Some blood dribbled down from his nose over the tape on his mouth. Two big men stood to either side of his chair. One had a pair of pliers out, poised to start pulling fingernails. A third man stood at the light switch, his expression irritated.

I realized they all must have watched me climb through the window and then open the back door. I wondered what they had thought of it.

"I said," the third man snapped, "who the hell are you?" He had a thick Russian accent and more tats than I had ever seen outside of an Alcoholics Anonymous meeting.

Not knowing what else to do, I started with my pitch, "I'm Eddie Connors, this is Arnold Wreckt, we're here to talk with Norm Linus about starring in his next movie production."

"Well, *we* are talking to him, so piss off, kid," the Russian told me.

"Is there a problem?" Wreckt stepped forward.

The speaker looked over at his friends. "We don't have a problem, right, Alexei?"

"No, Ivan, there is no problem." Alexei was the one holding the pliers, and he stepped forward and bent them in half. Either he was a Talent, or he was BENT, or he had taken steroids from the womb.

"You're Ivan, then?" I asked their leader hopefully. "Look, I don't know why you all are here…"

I didn't get the chance to finish, because Ivan stepped forward and hit me.

He really shouldn't have done that. For one thing, I was trying to tell them that we didn't want any trouble and would be leaving.

For another, basically the second he hit me, Wreckt returned the favor.

I stood up, my whole face hurting. Ivan had hit the fridge door, gone through it, and then taken the fridge through the wall and into the garage.

Their captive's eyes had gone wide over the strip of tape.

Alexei let out a curse, and Ivan's other friend drew a hand cannon. Alexei charged forward, and then things went really crazy.

Alexei swung at Wreckt, and my friend caught the punch with his face. I say caught, because Alexei's fist hit him square in the teeth, and I heard a sound kind of like a boneless ham being dropped from a great height.

Alexei began to scream, clutching at his shattered hand, just as the other guy brought up his gun. "No, no, no!" I threw myself in front of him. "Not my paycheck!"

I am not entirely certain what I was trying to do. I mean, getting shot several times was certainly not going to help in regard to getting us a job.

The guy wasn't impressed with my attempt to stop him. He opened up point-blank into my chest.

Getting shot hurt about as much as I thought it would. I had a few things to compare it against as well. He shot five, maybe six times, and then Wreckt reached out, caught his wrist, and ripped his arm off.

Of course, at that point, I fell over. I had been reliably told that was what people did when they were shot.

"Ow, ow, ow, shit," I grunted and coughed blood.

I rolled over, feeling the bullet holes on my chest and seeing all the blood. I wanted to pass out or go into shock so it didn't hurt anymore. No such luck. Instead, I coughed, coughed again, and then gagged and hocked a bullet out of my lung and then out my throat, spitting it out.

"Ah… that sucks." I spat a big wad of blood and phlegm.

"Are you okay, Eddie?" Wreckt asked.

"I'm great," I gasped. "Never better."

I wasn't gushing blood anymore. That was either good or bad. Poking at the holes in my chest, I could see they had already sealed over. It all hurt. Like, hurt a lot.

I spat blood again and sat up, not sure if I was still spitting up blood from the lungs or if I had bit through my tongue to keep from screaming. My shirt was ruined. I pulled it off, seeing five bullet holes in the front and four in the back. "Nice shot grouping," I coughed hoarsely.

That Russian wasn't in a state to really hear anything I said. Having your arm ripped off at the shoulder probably contributed to that. Alexei had either gone into shock or something, his face pale, seated on the floor, staring at the floppy bits of his hand and arm. From how everything was drooping and bending in ways it shouldn't, I would guess he had shattered every bone in his hand and forearm.

"Help out our producer," I told Wreckt.

He peeled the tape off the hostage's mouth.

I started in on the pitch, "So, Linus, we're here because…"

"Look, I tried to tell them, you got the wrong guy, my name is Wallace Ritchie, I just rented this place as a vacation rental," the man babbled.

I stood shakily, feeling weak and a bit light-headed. "May I?" I asked politely, pointing at the wallet in his pocket.

"Please!" Wallace told me. "I tried to get them to look, they wouldn't, they kept saying that they knew they had the right place."

I pulled out his wallet. "Wallace Ritchie, from Des Moines, Iowa… you even have a Blockbuster

Video card in here, you really need to clean this thing out."

I nodded at Wreckt. "Help him free."

Wreckt wasn't all that gentle ripping the tape free, but Wallace seemed like the type just to be happy he wasn't having Alexei and Ivan use pliers on his fingernails. "Okay, you rented this place, do you have an address for the owner, anything like that?"

He shook his head. "It was a rental service. Man, my buddy told me I was crazy to take a vacation rental in Chicago. I wish I had listened to him. I'm going to ask for my money back."

"Yeah, you probably should do that." I looked around at the mess. "Might be hard to get the deposit back, though."

This was definitely not what I had wanted. At least none of these guys were in a state to come after us or anything. Hopefully, we could just get out of here and avoid any other issues.

"Okay, we're going to, uh, go," I told Wallace. "I mean, if you want to call the cops, we'd appreciate it if you didn't give them too many details on us."

Wreckt nodded. "We would really appreciate it."

Wallace looked up at him and then over at me. "Yeah, I, uh, didn't get a good look at the guys, they sounded, uh, Chinese? Yeah, Chinese. There were like eight of them."

"Sure, thanks, Wallace," I told him. I nodded at Wreckt. "Let's go, buddy."

We went out the back door, Wreckt gently shutting it behind us. We went back over the wall. I grabbed my roller suitcase from the bushes where I had stashed it, and Wreckt got his as well. Then, I led the way down the street about as fast as I could. My chest still hurt. I probably needed to swap my clothes for some without blood and holes. The streetlights were starting to come on, and in this neighborhood, I didn't want to attract any more attention by changing clothes in public.

It probably wouldn't do to get arrested for indecent exposure in proximity to the place we had technically broken into and then killed two guys. Granted, it was self-defense. I was sure the police wouldn't listen to that. They had never listened to me before, after all.

I was in a foul mood. We hadn't wanted any trouble, why didn't people just listen? It wasn't like it would take *that* long to hear what I had to say. No one ever listened. If some assholes had just listened to me when I was a kid, none of this would have happened. Wreckt would have the career he should have, I might have gotten a fair shake…

It frustrated me to no end that, once again, we had nowhere to go.

"That was our only lead, right?" Wreckt asked me as we walked.

"I know," I snapped. I paused then. "I'm sorry, Arnold. Are you okay, by the way?"

"I'm fine, never felt better," he told me. "You are the one who got shot."

"Yeah, I noticed that." I snorted, and my fingers went to the bloody holes in my shirt. Healing from injuries had been a part of me being BENT. It was just something that I dealt with. This had happened faster than before, though. "Maybe you aren't the only one to get a glow-up."

I wasn't sure how I felt about that. I'd been trapped in the body of a sixteen-year-old for the past thirty years. If I had a Talent now, would that change? Would I start reverse aging or something equally crazy? I could only imagine how bad it would be to be walking around like a five-year-old, trying to get people to listen to me.

I had thirty years trapped at sixteen. It sucked. The idea of it getting worse frankly terrified me.

I did know what I wanted to do about it. "Let's go get a drink."

Chapter 4

"Can you believe this crap?" One of the bar patrons waved at the TV as we came in. It had been a long walk to the nearest open bar. I had missed the bus stop, and my crappy cell phone had issues with the maps here in Chicago. Neither of us had the money for even a ride-share, so we had walked.

"Gotta be a publicity stunt for a new movie." The bartender shook his head, looking up at the screen. Kurt Russel had just done a superhero landing on what looked like an airfield, and the local news station cut over to some talking heads with a background of fire trucks with flashing lights.

"Russel is doing action flicks again?" I asked as I took a seat at the bar, and Wreckt sat down next to me. "That's awesome, he's good people." I thought he was a little long in the tooth, but he was one of the handful of decent people in Hollywood. If I had known he was doing a movie, I probably would have reached out to him as Wreckt's agent.

The television swapped over to some grainy video of the actor fighting some thug. He looked younger than he had in years. "Man, I never would have thought he'd go for the whole plastic surgery thing, but he looks great."

"Twenty-one or older, kid." The bartender pointed at me, at a sign above the bar saying they didn't serve minors, and then at the door. "Hit the road."

"I'm forty-five, jackass." I pulled my ID out of my wallet and showed him.

"I don't want to see your fake ID, take a hike, or I'll call the cops." The bartender was still looking up at the television.

"What is the problem?" Wreckt asked him. "He's my agent."

"I don't care if he's your personal bodyguard, he can't sit at the bar. I'll lose my license." The bartender scowled at him. "Get out of here, or I'll call the cops."

"I'll be right over there, okay?" I grumbled and went over to a table away from the bar, over in the back corner. "Happy?"

He ignored me and went back to watching the news.

Arnold Wreckt came over and sat down next to me. The bartender had made it clear he wasn't going to serve either of us, and this didn't seem like the kind of place to have quick or efficient wait staff. I had really wanted a drink, and now my stomach twisted and growled with hunger. Apparently, regenerating from multiple gunshots burned a lot of calories. I ignored the hunger and focused on the essentials. For now, I just needed someplace to sit down while I thought through our next move.

"Damn, whatever movie they're doing, they have some great special effects," I muttered as pieces of debris went flying as someone plowed through an aircraft on the television screen. "What do you think?"

"He's a good actor, and I like him." Wreckt scratched at his square jaw as he watched. "I hope his new movie does well."

I scowled at him. "Not *that*, do you think I should ask him if he has a spot for you? He got you as an extra a couple of times in his movies, even when almost no one else would touch you. I bet if we called him up—"

I broke off as several men came into the bar, moving fast. They wore jogging suits and had black masks over their faces, and every one of them carried an AK. At least, I thought they were AKs, I was a little fuzzy on firearms outside of movies.

One of the patrons started to move toward the back door, and one of the thugs hit him in the back hard with his rifle butt, and he went down. I kept very, very still. I didn't know what this was, and I didn't want any part in it.

"Alright, we're looking for two guys." The leader for them spoke with a heavy Russian accent.

Oh, this isn't good, I thought and shot a look at Wreckt. His expression shifted to something harder, and I saw the muscles on his arms tense.

"They killed two of Anton Karmazov's men tonight, the third one is in hospital," the man went on, walking down the length of the bar. I didn't think they had seen us in the back corner, not yet. The back door was only a few feet away. I gestured at Arnold, and I slowly stood up. He followed suit, and we slowly started moving for the back door.

"There is big man and short one. We know they are here, because one of our men followed them," the leader went on. "The man who tells me where to be finding them will be rewarded. Anyone who hides them, I will kill."

As one, the bartender and patrons pointed over in our direction.

I was halfway to the back door when the five goons looked over at us. "Son of a…"

"Get them." The leader waved.

His goons rushed forward, and I waved at Wreckt not to fight them.

"Look"—I gave them my biggest, friendliest smile—"I think there's been some kind of misunderstanding. Maybe we can talk about this?"

They grabbed me by the arms and legs and carried me out of the bar feet first. They didn't have much luck picking up Wreckt, I saw, but he walked along between two of them.

I cocked my head around. "Our stuff, hey, don't leave our suitcases behind!"

They got us in the back of an SUV, Russian rap blaring so loud, I could barely hear myself think. Craning my head, I saw one of them throw our roller bags into the back.

I had two AKs pointed at my face, so I kept my mouth shut. Mostly.

I couldn't help a snort as they put Wreckt in the seat next to me and the whole vehicle leaned over hard under his weight. "You've been putting on some pounds, Arnold."

"I can't help it." He patted his chiseled abs. "I probably need to work out some more."

Either the Russians didn't get the humor, or they didn't think we were funny. There was no accounting for taste.

Two big men got in on either side of us, squishing us together, and I could hear the SUV's shocks protest.

"Do you think it's rated for all this weight back here?" I groaned. "Maybe one of you could go the next row back? I'll do it if you want."

The one to my side slapped the back of my head, and I shut up.

They had to struggle to shut the doors, and I felt like they slammed all the air out of my lungs when they finally got the doors closed with the four of us in the back seat.

"Seatbelts for safety?" I coughed.

"Shut your mouth, dog," the leader said from the front seat. "Anton Karmazov wants you two alive to talk. That does not mean we cannot beat you within an inch of your life."

I wasn't about to tell him that I'd probably heal from the beating. One, because it was none of his business, and two, because that would still hurt a lot while they did it. Instead, I wisely kept quiet.

Who says that I don't know when to keep my mouth shut?

It wasn't a long drive, though it felt like it took forever, the loud Russian rap music making my head hurt and the tight confines of the back seat with the two goons squishing Wreckt and I into one another. By one another, I mean squishing me. Arnold was built like a brick wall, and there was about as much give to his flesh as there was to steel. I think I dislocated my spine jammed between him and a heavily muscled goon.

The interior of the SUV smelled of cheap vodka and heavy body odor with dashes of body spray. Combined with the driving, I started to feel nauseous.

The driver was either drunk or just not very good at driving. He kept hitting curbs and crossing the median and rumble strips. Now and again, a car would whip past, horn honking, and he would curse loudly in Russian over the sound of the rap or occasionally put down the window and give someone the finger.

When we finally pulled to a stop, he parked us at an angle on the curb, half in the street. A moment later, the goon on my side got out and pulled me out with him. Wreckt slid out behind me, the shocks groaning as he did so.

We were in front of some kind of warehouse that had been converted into a club. A line of people were gathered out front, and several more goons in tracksuits played bouncer.

Our captors hustled us inside and onto a crowded dance floor.

The inside of the club was impressive, and I had seen a lot of this stuff over the years working in the film industry. Someone had replaced a big part of the roof with a skylight, there was a huge bar along the side, flashing lights, and sound and noise that hammered at me. I didn't much like the music, but I could dig all the people having fun. There was enough bass that my intestines loosened up, and I felt like I needed to use the bathroom.

Halfway across the dance floor, a twenty-something woman danced up toward our group. "Hey, I recognize you, you're Arnold Wreckt, like, get Wreckt, man!"

"Hey, brand recognition, I like it!" I waved at her as I went past, and she took a selfie with us in the background. "See, big guy, you still have fans."

"My mom had *such* a crush on you," she gushed at her friends. "This is so awesome, who wants some more ex?"

Well, so much for asking her for any help, I thought to myself.

Wreckt shouted at me as the goons moved us along, "Shouldn't we be worried about this?" He gestured at the goons around us.

"We'll work this out, I'm sure of it," I assured him. We were going to get our movie made, I was going to help Wreckt pull his career back. This was just a bump in the road. Surely, this Anton guy would realize it was all a misunderstanding. In fact, maybe he even knew where we could find Linus.

They led us up a set of stairs and through a door into a soundproofed office that overlooked the dance floor. There was a desk the size of a Cadillac taking up the center of the office, all glass and metal and hard lines. The furniture was all glass, too, fancy and expensive stuff. There were some designer chairs, too, with some people seated in them.

"Hey, nice place, guys. I mean, this is perfect, I can tell you all have put a lot of work into it. It's like right out of a movie set…"

One of the goons elbowed me in the stomach. "Shutting up, now," I gasped.

"Vasily, when I told you bring them to club, I meant basement." The boss was a big man with hard features and a serious expression. He wore a suit, unlike most of his men, and he was seated behind the big desk, with his back to the windows on the dance floor.

"Sorry, Mister Karmazov, I did not realize you had guests," our lead captor answered. *Vasily, the boss called him Vasily.* It was important to remember names, people paid attention when you talked to them by name.

"Business," the man sighed. I assumed he was Anton Karmazov, since that was the name they had used before. Anton looked over at his other guests. The first one sort of looked like a goblin and a zombie got it on and had a love-child with all the worst attributes of both. The second one was a man whose jowls had jowls. He was like the personification of glutton. He reminded me instantly of Harvey Moore. He had the same slick sort of arrogance and smugness about him.

"What the fuck are they?" I asked sotto voce. I assumed they were both BENT or something.

I got another elbow in the stomach for my troubles, and I shut up.

"… as I was saying," Anton went on, "I hope that none of today's issues impact my business plans?"

"No, Mister Karmazov," the goblin-zombie told him. "The City of Chicago has no issues with your legitimate business interests. If anything, some of the damage ties in well with the peaceful protests we had as far as clearing out any last holdouts over the property acquisitions."

"Similarly," the fat man groaned, "the State of Illinois has no problems with you and your associates. We, of course, would not dream of impeding such a distinguished and accomplished businessman, especially not with your regular contributions to the State of Illinois's Union Pension Funds."

"Excellent, excellent." Anton looked over at us. "These are men who hurt Petrov and killed the others?"

"Yes, boss." Vasily nodded and shoved me forward.

I smiled and turned on the charm. I could talk my way out of this, I knew it. "I can explain, it's a simple misunderstanding—"

Anton pulled a huge pistol out of his desk and shot me in the face.

If you've never felt the sensation of your brains being blown outwards in a shockwave as a metal slug slams through your skull… well, you aren't missing much. It hurt. A lot. Then it didn't. The good news was I didn't have to poop anymore. The bad news was that the bullet literally scrambled my brains, and the world pretty much stopped while my Talent knit everything back together.

Understandably, I sort of lost track of things there for a few moments.

When I did come to, there was a lot of screaming and yelling. I sat up just as Wreckt threw Vasily through the office window and up through the skylight. From the angle and velocity, the Russian might make low Earth orbit.

The little goblin-zombie thing tripped over me, and I tangled up with her as I tried to stand.

She screamed in my face and hit me. "Stop attacking me, hate-crime, hate-crime!"

"What the hell?" I tried to get my hands up to protect myself.

Her fat companion stepped right on my nuts as he ran for the door. I let out a shout and curled up into a ball of agony. I somehow managed to trip him, and he went down on top of the little goblin, both of them screaming in panic.

Another goon leveled his weapon in my direction, and Wreckt threw a metal-and-glass chair at him. The legs of the chair punched through his torso and into the wall behind him and spattered blood pretty much everywhere.

"Stop killing people!" I shouted at Wreckt.

"Sorry, I meant to just knock him down," Wreckt called back. A goon hit him in the back with another chair, and glass exploded everywhere. Wreckt caught the goon and threw him forward over his shoulder and through the bit of window that he hadn't already broken.

I caught a glimpse of Anton Karmazov running out a side door, and the fat man and goblin had run out the other door. It was really time to go. One of Karmazov's late and unlamented goons had left a good-sized hole in the wall thanks to Wreckt, and I led the way through, trying not to think about the wet, squishy sensation of what was underfoot in the next room.

There was a fire escape door just down the hall, and I ran that way. Pushing through it, I jumped over the railing of the fire escape and dropped to the ground.

I had misjudged the height. It was probably a twenty foot drop to the pavement, and my ankles broke with an audible and painful crunch. "Oh, damn. That always worked in the movies."

Wreckt came over the railing, and I tried to shout a warning. He landed on the dumpster next to me, pounding the steel lid down and splitting the side, spraying me with refuse, somehow walking out of it looking fine. I could feel the bones in my legs fusing back together and into place, and I did the smart thing and dropped to the ground, writhing in pain.

I wasn't sure if I was healing faster or if I just hadn't been hurt all that much before. It sure felt like an eternity before my legs stopped hurting enough for me to stand up.

"Let's go," I gasped as I got up and started limping toward the street. I was covered in refuse, blood, and I had shit my pants. I probably looked like some kind of vagrant. I wanted a shower and a change of clothes. More importantly, I didn't want to get shot anymore.

There were dozens of people out in the street, flooding out of the club, many of them yelling and screaming. Fire alarms were going off in the club. I heard police sirens in the distance.

One of the goons was still at the SUV on the curb, and as I limped up, he saw me.

"Hey, yeah, your boss said we could go. This was all just a crazy misunderstanding." I limped closer, smiling as ingratiatingly as I could and hoping he even understood English.

He squinted at me, looked at Wreckt coming behind me, and went for his gun.

Wreckt stepped forward, caught him, and threw him across the street. He bounced off the brick face of that warehouse and flopped to the ground, unconscious or dead. I kind of didn't care at this point.

I sighed. "I tried, I really tried." That left no other goons around the SUV. It was just standing there, engine running. "Oh, well, get in." I tried to do a cool slide over the hood and just managed to thump into the side of it with my hip and fall to the pavement. I got up and limped around it instead.

"I thought you didn't have a license." Wreckt frowned at me as he climbed in. I could feel the SUV lean over under his weight.

"My license got revoked, yeah," I told him. I had a state-issued identity card from California. It was part of the agreement that had got me out of jail as a teenager, and I hadn't ever gone back to get a driver's license after all that fell off my record. "It'll be fine. Besides, our bags are in the back. We can't stick around here, or this is just going to get more complicated."

I put it in drive and pulled forward, the crowd parting around me as I crawled us away. "See? No problem."

I looked in the rearview mirror as a group of goons rushed out of the club, pointing in our direction as we pulled away. "Hah, assholes, we have your car, sucks to be you!" I put the driver window down and flipped them the bird as I pulled away.

Behind us, I heard gunfire, and a bullet ripped through the back window and punched through the windshield in front of me. "Yeah, I probably shouldn't have done that."

"We need to get out of here." Wreckt looked over his shoulder at the goons behind us.

"Still not a problem. They don't have vehicles. We're good," I assured him as I accelerated away.

In my side mirror, I saw the goons had rushed over to two SUVs. They both roared to life, even as the Russians continued to fire at us. Russians piled in, and the two cars began to pursue us.

"Okay, something of a problem." I gunned the gas, and the wheels screamed as the SUV leaped forward.

Get Wreckt

Chapter 5

I drove us around the corner, tires squealing, and right past two cop cars and a fire truck with their lights flashing and sirens wailing. "Look, the cops, see, we're good, man," I told Wreckt.

Driving right behind us came two more SUVs with goons and AKs firing at us.

In my rearview, I could see the two cop cars shut their lights off and keep driving the other way. I could practically hear them saying "Nope, nope, not gonna get involved in that shit."

"Thanks, guys, that's really helpful." I ducked as gunfire ripped through the car, smashing the rearview mirror.

I drove faster, bullets ripping toward us. In the movies, bullets bounced off cars. In real life, I could hear them snap through the back hatch and punch through seats and then right out the front windshield. Not in front of Wreckt, though. I could see bullets bouncing off him. Bits of shrapnel tore into me, lancing little bits of pain that made my hands jerk on the steering wheel and made us swerve as I drove.

"Get behind me," I told Wreckt. He was bulletproof, then maybe anything that hit him wouldn't go through to punch through me.

He climbed over the seat and got behind me. It threw the balance of the SUV off, and it was all I could do not to roll it. I got control, steadied it out, and went as fast as I could. Gunfire continued to roar behind us, and bullets smashed the console into a sparking ruin.

The SUV started to lose power. I guided it to the side, the gas feeling mushy, the engine roaring, but the vehicle continuing to slow.

I managed to pull to the side as the two SUVs came alongside, the men aboard leveling weapons at us.

"Oh shit." I bailed out of the still-moving vehicle as they opened up.

Wreckt jumped too, and the two of us bounced and skidded, me leaving patches of skin and blood behind while he ripped up chunks of pavement.

"I got our bags," Wreckt told me, holding up the two roller suitcases, even as the two cars full of goons continued to fire into our SUV as it rolled to a stop about a block away. I pointed down the alleyway next to us, and we ran that way.

"Okay, clearly, we need to reprioritize," I told him as we hurried along. Every step hurt as my skin knitted itself back together.

"Are you okay?" Wreckt asked me. "I saw them shoot you. Like, in your head. There were brains and other things."

"Yeah, yeah." I tried not to think about it. "I'm fine."

I felt like if Morgan Freeman were narrating my life, he would say "But he wasn't fine." I had felt my brains being blown out of the back of my head. It had really hurt. I didn't think that was *supposed* to hurt. Someone had told me once that brains didn't have nerves in them, that you shouldn't feel pain from a brain injury. Maybe I had imagined it, but it sure as hell felt real. I was pretty sure that I probably needed to talk to a shrink or go on an alcohol-infused bender. Or something.

I stank. It was a funk of sweat, nasty garbage, and the filth from my own bowels.

"I wish I had my phone," I muttered. I had lost my cheap cell phone in the chaos somewhere back at the club.

"I got Vasily's." Wreckt passed it to me.

"How?" I asked.

"He dropped it when I threw him through the skylight. It seemed like something useful to grab." Wreckt shrugged. "I don't think he'll need it anymore."

"Yeah, I don't think they have cell phone reception in orbit." I laughed. "Okay, let's see… shit, this thing is in Russian, one second…" It took me a minute to switch the language over and then pull up a map. The first thing I was going to do was find us a bus station or train station or something and get us out of town.

I stopped, though, as I saw several pins that he had dropped on the map. One was Norm Linus's house. The other was marked as his office. It wasn't too far. It sort of was on the way to the train station.

"We're going to make a little detour," I told Wreckt.

We stopped by a place that rented rooms by the hour. The manager gave us a nasty smirk as I got a key. I didn't care. I looked and smelled like literal shit. I wanted to make use of the facilities and change clothes. Of course, both of our roller bags had taken multiple bullet hits, and all my shirts had holes punched through them.

I hosed off the worst of the filth and blood in the shower then made room for Arnold. He took longer to shower than me, but his body was like four times as big, so I didn't begrudge him the time.

Vasily's phone was a much newer and nicer model than mine. It even had a handy feature for transferring accounts to a new device, and I got everything moved over and logged into my email with no issues. Vasily had a bunch of other contacts in there, too, but I left those for now. Who knew, maybe Anton Karmazov had some Hollywood contacts? I would have to check when I had more time.

Once we were both cleaned and dressed, I confirmed the address for Norm Linus's office, and we checked out of the hotel with a few seconds left on the clock as I turned over the key. The manager gave me a sneer as I walked away, and I could give two shits what he thought.

We walked the quarter mile to Norm's office building. The front lobby had a security guard, but the guy was playing video games on his cell phone and didn't even look up as we came in. Thankfully, it looked like the kind of place where people worked late, and we hustled past the guard and over to the elevators.

I saw a light on in the office as we came out of the elevator. As I went up to the door and knocked, the light went out.

"Mister Linus, I know you're there. We're here to talk to you about making a movie." I kept my voice as confident as I could manage.

The light came back on, and a moment later, he opened the door. He was heavy-set, with big thick glasses and a short beard. "You are?"

"Yes, I'm Eddie Connor, you probably don't remember me. Anyway, I am Arnold Wreckt's agent…"

"Actors." Linus slammed the door in my face.

"You don't understand," I protested at the closed door. "I think he could be a stand-in for your next movie!"

Norm Linus opened the door and squinted at me from behind his glasses, "*You* don't understand. There won't be a next movie. I've been blacklisted by Hollywood for forty years! The pedophile, commie, fascist bastards wouldn't let me make a commercial!"

"I can deeply empathize," I told him. "Look, we were over at your home earlier today—"

"Is that why the vacation renter wanted a refund?" Linus frowned.

"I can't really say," I hedged. "Look, can we at least come into your office and talk?"

Linus looked at me and then at Wreckt and sighed. I heard a click, and he stepped away from the door and shoulder-holstered a huge pistol of some kind that he had been holding out of sight.

It made me wonder if everyone in Chicago was packing guns except for me. I thought this city had gun control or something. *He's a legitimate guy, he's probably got a permit,* I told myself.

"Yeah, sure." He swung the door wide. "Come on in."

He was wearing a khaki vest, the kind that old fishermen and hunters wore, and short khaki shorts. I giggle-snorted a bit at the look, thinking he looked like he was going to go on safari.

There wasn't much of an office. He had a cluttered desk covered in loose papers and a number of old and obsolete cameras. He had a cheap couch against one wall with a rumpled blanket thrown on it, which told me he was sleeping here while he rented out his house. The office windows looked out on the brick wall of the adjacent building.

His eyes went wide behind his glasses as he saw Wreckt in the light. "Holy smokes, you must have got some serious work done. What did you take? Human growth hormones?"

"I just work out, exercise regularly, and eat well," Wreckt told him.

"Yeah, so do I, and I look like shit." Linus shook his head. He gave me a nod. "Alright, kid, so, your client looks like a movie star again, I'll give you that. Hell, if he had something of a career and notoriety before this, I would have wagered you've been flying him overseas to China for stem cell treatments."

"What now?" I asked with a frown.

"Oh, the little parts of China that's still around, the ones that got in bed hard with the Russkies, those Soviet commie fucks. Anyway, they started farming their political prisoners. They got this horrifying thing going where if you talk nice about them in the media and pay more money than any of us will ever see, they run aborted fetus stem cells through your blood and swap out any organs that aren't doing so hot from political prisoners. Really nasty setup. I ran a documentary on it, some Hollywood types and politicians lost their minds because I named names, and not even the indie producers would touch it. That was the final straw, that's why I'm here in Chicago. They ran me right out of California."

"That sounds awful." I stared at him. I really hoped it was some kind of conspiracy theory. Stuff like that didn't happen for real… right?

"Anyway, just another group to hate my guts." Linus pushed his glasses up and rubbed his eyes. "I got turned on to another documentary, about how the politicians in this crooked state are pushing those damned riots to burn out small businesses and how the Russian mob is picking up real estate cheap. Some conservative think tank is footing the bill for me to dig up the story and do a documentary on it. I'm not doing entertainment movies, I haven't for decades."

"I was going to do that barbarian movie with you," Wreckt told him.

"Yeah, after your Olympians of California flop." Linus shook his head. "We never could line up the funding for that one either. That was forty years ago, man."

"Look, what do we need to make a movie?" I asked him as I put a business card down in front of him.

"Investors, a director, producer, script, actors, extras, stunt coordinator, soundtrack, leading star, and some eye candy." Linus ticked off on his fingers. "Filming location, sets, costumes, props…"

"Okay, you got that conservative think tank, maybe you can line up someone else, too?" I asked. "I mean, look at Arnold, he's a star, man!"

"I remember you now." Linus shook his finger at me. "You were that little pipsqueak that got Harvey Moore punched in the face… and the one doing the punching was Arnold Wreckt, right?"

"He had it coming," Wreckt spoke in an ominous tone.

"See, great actor," I assured Linus. "Look at that expression."

"Harvey Moore is a shitweasel, pinko-commie, he deserved what he got and worse." Linus sniffed. "I meant to track you down and shake both your hands over that, but you just sort of disappeared."

My parents had plied me up with a bunch of drugs, my agent had tried to set up something to save my career, and I had ended up on a drug-fueled bender that had got me arrested. Then things had *really* gone bad when my career had fallen apart. I didn't say any of that, though. "Yeah, things got a little crazy there for a while. I got out of acting. I'm Arnold's agent, now."

"Well, I suppose…" Linus sighed. "Yeah, for sticking it to that prick, I probably owe you both to at least give it a try. Just so we're straight, though, if I agree to do this, I run it my way, agreed?"

"Of course." I nodded. I didn't have the slightest idea what I was doing.

"Fine." Linus shook his head. "I can't believe I'm saying this, but I am in. I know just the leading lady. I know an actress in town. She lives in northern Chicago. Here's her address." He scribbled it down on one of his random sheets of paper.

This was moving so quickly that I just took it, too excited to protest at being made his errand-boy. *We're doing it, we're going to make a movie,* I thought to myself. Arnold Wreckt would get his chance at stardom, I would be able to take care of the pair of us, and we would show the people who had thrown us away that they had been wrong.

Norm Linus went on, "Good, now, we need to get a—"

Someone kicked in the door.

Three men hurried into the room. They were black, so I assumed they weren't Russians at least.

The one at the lead spoke, "Look, mother, you been told to stop your interviews…"

The speaker, a short black guy with lots of gold chains and saggy pants, trailed off, his chin going up as he looked at the looming form of Wreckt. His head went up, then up further, and still higher. "Shit, you a grass-fed homeboy."

"Do you have an appointment?" Wreckt loomed over him. He was really good at looming when he wanted to, and I could see the lead thug sort of wilt down a bit like a plant out in the sun with no water.

"Yo, dawg, we don't need an appointment, we got guns." He brandished a gold-plated pistol and seemed to have found his courage. He smirked at me. He had a grill, which I thought weren't in fashion anymore.

"I think there's a misunderstanding here." I smiled back at him, trying to be as disarming as possible. Especially since they were armed and I wasn't.

Behind me, I heard a metallic thunk as Linus drew a shotgun from behind his desk and racked the slide.

There were suddenly a lot of guns aimed at me and through me. I wasn't interested in any of that, but I didn't dare move. "Uh, look, guys, we're just here to make a movie."

"A movie?" the short black guy asked suspiciously. "That's why we're here, yo, that guy been talking to people, and he needs to stop. Powerful people want him gone!"

"Look, I don't know anything about that. What I do know is we're making an action movie," I told him. "This is Arnold Wreckt, he's my client, and I'm his agent. He's an actor, he does action movies."

"Never heard of him," the short one said.

"He's sort of up and coming," I told him. "Anyway, we're here to sign Mister Linus on as the producer and director. We're just about to go get some of the other people we need to make the movie. You know, a set, a script…"

"I wrote a script," one of the two thugs blurted.

"You wrote a script?" His boss turned his head. "Man, not this crap again, not right now."

"Is it any good?" Linus asked from behind me.

"My momma liked it," the thug told us.

The leader of the thugs rounded on him, "Man, who cares what your momma…"

Wreckt hit the little guy, not hard, but enough that he flew into the hallway and stopped talking.

"What is this script about?" Wreckt asked.

The other thug wisely lowered his weapon while the one with the script started talking, "So, it's this period piece, yo, about this queen, and she is, like, super fine, you know, but she got problems. She needs a man, like, a serious man, to solve them."

"That could be pretty good," I said. "What's your name?"

"C-dawg," he told me. He looked at his buddy as if he were embarrassed and then blurted, "Uh, my name is Clarence."

"Look, Clarence, how about you and Mister Linus talk through the details on the script," I offered him. "He's the guy who did the *Bullets, Blades, and Babes* movies."

"No shit, man? I watched every one of those movies, like, five times," Clarence gushed. "That one scene when the robot chick with machine gun tits smokes all those dudes in the strip club, that was off the hook, man."

"Well"—Linus smiled and finally lowered his shotgun—"I'm actually pretty proud of that scene. It really showed the duality of sex and violence."

Clarence nodded. "Yeah, man, and the way the music and the light worked, and when you faded to black and white except for the blood from the dudes… just really made that whole sequence pop." They started getting into additional details, and I tuned them out.

I was a former actor and now agent; I'd never really been into actually watching or appreciating movies, just the business of making them. Honestly, I couldn't remember the last time I had even *watched* a movie, either on television or in theaters. Hanging around on set, pitching Arnold Wreckt, and getting my foot in the door to get him roles, that had been what I liked.

The money, too, of course. I really liked that.

I looked over at the other thug who had been doing his best to fade into the office wallpaper after what happened to his boss. I noticed he was a pretty big guy, too, not as big as Wreckt, but buff and not bad looking. "Who are you?"

"Name's Trev… man."

"You do any acting?" I asked.

"Nah, man, I just do work for Little Tee," he told me, pointing at where Wreckt had knocked his erstwhile employer into the hallway. "He's a bookie most of the time, and he runs a weed grow on the side. When someone owes money, he and I come and threaten them until they pay up. Occasionally, we do work for his aunt. She's really connected, so that keeps the heat off us."

I squinted at him. "Does that pay well?"

"I get a solid 5 percent when I convince folks to pay up what they owe," Trev told me.

"I mean, we're making a movie, I know the director. If you want someone to represent you, I can get you a good deal, maybe even a speaking role," I told him.

"You really think I could do something like that?" Trev seemed surprised.

"Yeah, and the best part is, as your agent, *I* would be the one getting a percentage, you'd be getting the rest. I only get paid when you earn money." I pulled out my wallet and slid out a business card. "Think about it."

He took the card, and I started for the door. I was still holding the paper with the address on it for our leading actress. I took a moment to put it in the phone. It wasn't anywhere near us, and I wasn't looking forward to walking or taking a bus that far.

I looked up from the cell phone. "Oh, hey, Trev, do you have a car?"

"Yeah, Little Tee has me drive him around." Trev nodded.

I shook my head. "You only get 5 percent, and you drive him in your personal vehicle? Look, man, we got to talk about your arrangements."

I cleared my throat, then, as I realized I probably hadn't helped myself. "Uh, do you mind giving us a ride? I need to go meet our leading lady," I told him.

"Sure, man." He was looking at my business card like someone had written him a check already. "Not a problem."

Chapter 6

We dropped Little Tee off at a hospital along the way. He wasn't in a shape to complain about it, what with a broken jaw, and all the rest.

Trev and Wreckt had spent most of the drive talking fitness. I guess Trev was a gym rat, which made sense with how he was built. They had compared diets, exercise regimens, and different muscle-building techniques that I had mostly tuned out. There was a whole lot of science and thought that went into what Wreckt and guys like him did, way more than I had ever cared to follow.

None of it mattered to me, of course. It didn't matter how much I ate or worked out, what I did, my body kept me pretty much stable.

We had pulled up in front of the house when I realized I didn't even have a name for our actress. Nor, I realized, had I remembered to get Norm Linus's phone number. At least I had given him a business card, so he would have my number to reach me. "Uh, Trev, you mind waiting here? I don't know how long we'll be…"

"Nah, man, we cool," Trev told me.

"Great, man." We had discussed what kind of roles he might fit, and he was thinking rapper or sports star. With how the business was, I might have more luck getting him roles as the gay best friend or something like that. At the least, I was sure I could get him in *this* movie.

We just needed a leading lady first.

I went up to the door. It was a decent house, and I wondered if she had paid for it herself. As an actress, she might need an agent, and I was always looking for new clients. I knocked and then glanced at my acquired phone and realized how late it was. "She's probably not even awake," I muttered.

"I'm awake, alright," I heard a raspy voice from the security camera doorbell. "Who the hell are you?"

"I'm Eddie, I'm an agent…"

The raspy woman laughed. "Sure you are, kid. Who's the lunk, your personal assistant?"

"This is Arnold Wreckt, my client. I'm representing him for a movie we're making with Norm Linus, who sent me over here to sign on a leading lady for the big budget movie he's making," I told her.

"Big budget?" The raspy woman laughed. "The only big budget Norm has is for his firearms. Ah, hell, come on in, kid, you've amused me enough to let you make your pitch."

The door buzzed, and I hurried in, followed by Arnold.

A doorman greeted us. He was huge, broad of shoulder, and I was going to guess Middle Eastern or Indian. I squinted at him. "Weren't you in some of those spy movies?" I asked him.

"Nah, I'm not an actor, I just take care of her," he told me with a light, friendly voice. In the foyer, I could see that he had the upper-body of a strongman, but the lower body didn't match, almost like he skimped on leg day.

"Huh, well if you ever want…" I slipped him a business card.

He took it with a laugh. "I appreciate it. My wife will find it amusing as well. I don't have the patience to deal with Hollywood types."

"Me either," I admitted.

He led us into a dining room with a bar along one side. An older woman, her face wrinkled, her body withered, but her posture straight, sat at the bar, a glass of amber liquid in one hand and an unlit cigarette in the other. "Thank you, Doctor Nik, for getting the door. I don't think I'm up to it at the moment."

She peered at me, her dark eyes glittering with interest. "Alright, then, let's hear about your movie." She didn't get up to greet us, and I couldn't blame her. She looked frail enough that I was worried she might fall over.

Wreckt looked at me, and I hiked my head over at where Doctor Nik had settled in next to the television. He went over, and they started talking about weight lifting.

I wasn't sure why Linus had sent us here. She didn't look like a leading lady, she looked one foot in the grave. Maybe she was the actress's grandmother or something?

I settled on the barstool next to her and pointed at the crystal decanter. "May I?"

"You old enough to drink, boy?" She rasped a laugh.

"I'm older than I look," I assured her.

She took a sip and shrugged. I poured. It was a bourbon—an expensive bourbon—and I savored its smoky flavor for a moment. "Woah, it has been a while. That's some *really* good stuff."

"Tell me about your movie." She sipped.

"It's a…" My brain froze up, and I completely forgot the sparse details that Clarence had given me. "It's an action flick," I told her, my mouth speaking before my brain could catch up.

"I am hardly surprised. That sounds like Norm Linus. Lots of guns, your ripped young man over there flexing muscles, probably a car chase or two, and some deeper theme about freedom or something, knowing Linus." Our hostess cackled. "Go on."

"There's a bodybuilder and his, uh…" I trailed off. "Personal trainer. They run afoul of some Russian mobsters while they're trying to get their big break." The words flowed out in a rush.

"Sounds more like an action comedy." She arched an eyebrow at me. "Very cliché."

"Yeah, well, there's also some crooked politicians involved," I hurried to add. "And the violence is over-the-top, the bodybuilder is, like, Talent-level."

"My, my." She *tsked* at me. "Norm Linus wants me to come out of retirement for *this*?" She didn't seem impressed.

"I'm not really sure. He sent us for a leading lady and…" I trailed off.

"Hah, tell me about it," she rasped, putting the unlit cigarette in her mouth. "Alright, kid, what's your story, your *real* story?"

"What do you mean?" I asked.

She leveled a look at me. "You know your bourbon, you talk like an experienced hand, you look like you're twelve—"

"Sixteen," I corrected her.

"You talk a good patter, but you and your friend have clearly seen better days." Our hostess talked around the unlit cigarette, her withered lips holding it in place with precision.

"Why do you say that?" I hedged. I had cleaned myself up. I shouldn't look *too* shady.

She took her unlit cigarette out of her mouth. "Honey, you have bullet holes in your shirt, and I can see dried blood under your fingernails."

I looked down. "Oh, right." I probably should have scrubbed a bit harder in the shower.

"Tell me, sweetie, what's a kid like you doing here talking to a gal like me?" She cackled another laugh. "How are you escorting around that hunk over there, pitching a movie script to me, and looking over your shoulder like you expect someone to come kicking in the door chasing you?"

I sighed. I really didn't want to go into all this. "I was a child actor."

"No shit, join the club." She gave her raspy laugh around the unlit cigarette.

"Rising star, doing real well." I shrugged. "If you were one, then you know how it goes. My parents had me strung out on more medications than a cancer ward and spent my earnings on houses in the Maldives."

My voice dropped into a monotone as I went on, "They saw me once a month and made sure the checks cashed. My agent was little more than a pimp, you know the type."

"Some shitweasel who made sure you had personal alone time with the producer?" she asked me in a sharp voice.

Apparently, she knew Hollywood well enough. "Yeah."

I took another sip of the bourbon. Alcohol didn't really affect me, neither did drugs. A side effect of my body regenerating. I could still appreciate the flavor.

I went on, my fingers trembling a little bit on the glass. "I kept things together pretty well until I got the role of a lifetime, one of the lead actors on *Roboslayer Three*…"

"Ah, shit, you're Eddie Connor." She shook her head. "I can't believe I didn't recognize you."

"Thanks, I guess I did make a lot of tabloids." I shook my head. "I was at a casting party, we were two months into filming, and Harvey Moore was the producer." Harvey had done the previous two *Roboslayer* movies, too, as director, producer, and writer. He had been the crème of Hollywood action movies at the time. "Harvey had been drinking and got handsy with just about everyone. When he grabbed me, I'd had quite a bit to drink on top of the meds my parents had me on. I had enough, so I shouted for him to get the hell off me."

I shrugged then. "He slapped me, right in front of God and everyone. He told me to be a good little boy and do what I was told." My knuckles went white on the glass, and I carefully set it down so I wouldn't break it.

I nodded over at where my friend was lifting the refrigerator one-handed as he pointed out small muscles in his arm with the other. "Wreckt was there, and he hit Harvey and broke his jaw. We both got canned. Wreckt got blacklisted. I went on a bender as my career went into a death-spiral, couldn't get much of anything for roles…"

"Yeah, last I remember, you went to rehab, and then there was a funeral or something." Our hostess shook her head. "Crazy fucking year that one was. Harvey Moore was a pig, though. He deserved punches and worse. A real equal-opportunity abuser. Too bad he makes good movies and kisses the right ass in Hollywood. No one will ever touch him."

I frowned. "Wait… I remember you." I couldn't remember where from, though; it was something of the sparkle of her green eyes that made me certain I knew her.

She arched an eyebrow at me. "Go on with your story, kid."

"Yeah, I kind of went on a bender, stole that car while being on enough cocaine to lift the space shuttle." I sighed. That had been a mistake, but I had been so angry with my parents and my doctors and the police. None of them had listened to me, they had all thought I was just some drugged-out kid. "Then there was the whole police chase."

"That made national news. You were going, what, a hundred and twenty?"

"One-thirty-five, right down Hollywood Boulevard." I couldn't help but smile.

"You're lucky you didn't kill anyone," she told me.

"I was trying to kill myself. No such luck." I shook my head. "Anyway, that was pretty much it for my acting career. My parents were trying to get me committed or something. They were freaking because their cash cow had imploded." I stared out the window over her shoulder at the darkness outside, not able to look at her as I went on.

"I got to a dark place, and then went a little darker. They left me home while they went somewhere, Spain, I think?" I let out a ragged, angry breath. "My dad left his gun cabinet unlocked and open and talked about the great insurance plan he had on me, one with suicide coverage and everything. You can guess that they were hoping what I would do."

"Did you?" She mouthed her unlit cigarette.

"Those things will kill you." I pointed at it.

"You're not joking." She laughed.

I sighed. "I should know, believe me." I shuddered as I thought back.

"I got a couple of cans of gasoline, poured them all over the house, all over me, and lit up a cigarette. It was about the worst fucking sensation I ever felt.

I could feel my hair and skin burn off, my lungs sear, my eyeballs burst…"

I picked up the glass and took a rather large sip of her bourbon. My hand shook so much, I nearly spilled it. "I was done. Dead. Gone. My parents got their insurance money on the house and on me. They cashed the check before my funeral."

I laughed. "Good thing for them, because I sat up out of the casket at the funeral, spitting out staples and screaming. My parents hopped a private jet to a non-extradition country and kept the insurance money." I held up a hand. "My horrific death triggered my BENT. I regenerated just as I was, sixteen years old, and I've stayed that way for the past twenty-nine years."

"Shit, Eddie, that sounds pretty bad." My hostess shook her head.

"That's it." I pointed at her as she said my name. "We were in a movie together… that cartoon ghost one. I played him when he got to be a live boy, and I got to be on-scene all of thirty seconds, I was… twelve, I think?" I snapped my fingers. "Katie Rocco, right?"

She spread her hands. "In the flesh."

"What the hell happened to you?" I asked in shock.

"Don't pull any punches, Eddie." Katie laughed.

"We are, like, almost the same age." I shook my head. "You look ninety years old."

"Similar life, Eddie, same types of assholes. I did less of the drugs, more of the self-abuse." She shrugged. "When I was sixteen, they diagnosed me with late-onset progeria, they think triggered by anorexia and stress."

"Pogen… What's that?" I asked.

"Progeria is a disease where you age rapidly. Normally, it triggers on birth, and the kid is lucky to get to ten years old. Occasionally, *very* rarely, it gets triggered later on in childhood. In three years, I went from sixteen to sixty." She shrugged. "I probably don't have to tell you what that did for my acting career."

"I've seen you in stuff, though." I frowned. "You were in a couple of Linus's movies, right?"

She took out a lighter and flicked it a couple times before seating her unlit cigarette in her mouth and then lighting it. "Like you said, these things will kill you." She laughed and sucked in smoke.

A moment later, she coughed and dropped the cigarette. She coughed more smoke, a gush of it. Her eyes widened. "You're going to *hate* this part," she gasped. A moment later, flames exploded out of her mouth. Fire consumed her, burning her hair and skin, roasting her from the inside out and back in, until she was nothing but a standing column of smoke and flame while I stared on in horror.

A moment later, as clouds of fine ash rained down, Doctor Nik came over with a broom and dustpan in one hand and a silk kimono in the other. "She's always leaving such a mess." He shook his head.

"She just… what the…"

The column of fire and smoke cleared, and she stood there, sans clothing. Her doorman passed her the kimono, and she pulled it around her. Where before her skin had been weathered and wrinkled, now she had smooth white skin. Her thin gray hair had become long raven locks, and her green eyes twinkled with mischief. She looked sixteen years old, and I couldn't help but remember the kiss we had shared on screen.

"I'm a phoenix," she told me. "I was terminal at nineteen. They gave me hours to live. I went out in the back of the hospital with some of my friends and went through some of the bucket list stuff, and they lit me a birthday cake. I went to blow out the candles, and my brittle hair caught fire… and then I was standing there like this."

"Holy shit." I shook my head. "That happens to you every time?"

Katie gave me a nod. "I've learned to control it. I can advance or hold my age at any given point. It saves the special effects and makeup crews a lot of time for casting me in period pieces or long-running movies. They can get me from girlhood up through elderly."

"That's crazy, you're, like, the opposite of me." I laughed. "Fucking hell, what a mess Hollywood made of us, right?"

She took a sip of her bourbon. "On that, I can agree with you, Eddie."

Behind us, Wreckt turned up the volume on the television. "Eddie, I think you need to see this."

We walked over. On the screen, I recognized the fat guy who'd stepped on my nuts and the little goblin-zombie who had tripped on me. "…these two are armed and dangerous. They should be treated with extreme caution. As I stated, earlier, while the mayor and I were at a business conference with some legitimate business interests in our fair city, these two men attacked us."

"They were screaming 'white power' at me when they did it," the goblin-zombie said into the microphone. "The little one actually grabbed me and said this is GAG country."

"What the hell?" I asked in shock. "What does that even mean?"

Katie looked over at me. "GAG, you know? Grow America Great? It's the slogan for that president that used to sell real estate."

"I haven't ever voted in an election," I admitted. "They all just seem like crooks."

They popped up pictures of us both. Mine was my booking photo from thirty years ago. A police officer stepped forward and spoke, "Eddie Connor has prior arrests for drug possession, felony grand theft auto, resisting arrest, and indecent exposure. Arnold Wreckt has no prior charges, but both men are wanted and, as the mayor and governor stated, are considered dangerous. We're asking the public to immediately call if they see either of them."

"They expunged those!" I yelled at the television. "Those records were supposed to be sealed." I had been sixteen when I had done that stuff; it all should have been on my juvenile record.

I didn't know what kind of charges we faced. I didn't know if they *could* charge us for anything.

That Anton Karmazov guy had been trying to kill us. He *had* shot me, right in the head. The mayor had tripped on me while running away, and in a fair world, I could probably get the governor for assault with his lard ass stepping on my balls.

I had forty-five years of experience, though, with how unfair the world could be.

Katie laughed. "So, this action flick, do you have an ending for it yet?"

Chapter 7

Katie let us borrow the keys to one of her cars, and Wreckt and I headed to meet Linus. Katie Rocco had his phone number, and I had texted him that we had signed her onto the movie. He had texted me to come back to the office, so I let Wreckt drive.

I didn't have a problem in the little Mazda Miata, but Arnold barely fit, and the poor car's engine stuttered and sputtered under his weight whenever he hit the accelerator.

I looked over at him as he drove. I realized that he and I hadn't really talked about any of this. "What do you think, Arnold?"

He frowned as he drove. "What about?"

"Should we just hook it north and drive to Canada?" I asked him. "Hop a plane from there to someplace tropical?"

He snorted. "I think there is a lake in the way."

I was fuzzy on the geography. "Yeah, I'm sure there's a bridge or ferry or something, smart guy. I mean should we leave all this behind?"

"I think your friend would want her car back," Arnold pointed out, even as he shifted and the engine stuttered under his weight.

I scowled at him. "You're dodging the question, man, just give it to me straight. Should we stay or should we go? What do you want out of this?"

He drove in silence for a moment, downshifting as we took a curve on the road, and the shocks groaned. "Remember the script for *Roboslayer Three*?"

That was a weird question. I had to think back, a *long* way back, for that one. "Yeah, I think so."

"I liked it, because before that movie, I always played the bad guy. Even in the first couple of *Roboslayer* movies, I was the killer robot. In that one, I acted as a protector."

"Yeah, reprogrammed to serve humanity and guarding me from the other killer robots, I remember." I couldn't help but shake my head. "Harvey is a jackass, but he had some cool script ideas."

"It was nice to be the hero." Arnold's voice remained serious. "Most of the time, as the big guy, I got cast as the thug or bruiser."

"I remember." That was how I had managed to get him any roles at all as his agent. His catchphrase

"You'll get Wreckt" had been his threat, most often thrown down before he fought the good guys. Typically, he lost not long after that.

"I would like to play a hero again," Arnold spoke musingly. "More than that, wouldn't it be nice to be the actual good guy?"

I frowned at that. "Do you think there really *are* heroes out there?" I had a low opinion of all of that. I had come out of my legally-mandated rehab with a really low opinion of people and a lot of first-hand experience to back that up. The past thirty years of acting as Arnold Wreckt's agent had not improved that opinion.

"There are supers," Arnold noted.

"Sure," I scoffed, "the ones the federal government didn't arrest, and the ones who didn't get sued into oblivion. Remember Doctor Fantastic? Last I heard, the guy he cured of leprosy sued him and won over the loss of his disability pay. Guy lost his house, his car, everything, and then the government arrested him for practicing medicine without a license."

"That doesn't mean that what he was doing wasn't good," Arnold pointed out.

"Good, bad, it doesn't matter much when his cellmate Bubba is playing the big spoon. The same can be said for both of us, Arnold. That fat bastard and little goblin have it out for us." I wanted to point out that the last time he had tried to do something good, namely, protecting me from that jackass Harvey, it had cost him his acting career. I kept my mouth shut, though, because he was the one person who had ever stood up for me.

"So, why are we going to meet Linus then?" Arnold asked me. "Why aren't we running to Canada already?"

I looked out the window. I didn't answer for a long moment. "I don't know. Maybe I'm tired of bending over and taking it. Maybe I'm tired of running away. Maybe I just want to see you make a great movie like you were going to before your career went down the toilet because of me," I bit it out, fighting back tears.

"Hey, Eddie, it's all good." He patted me on the shoulder. "We've had some pretty good times."

We had lived in shit-holes and barely scraped by. I had called in every favor I had to try and get his fitness show, and then even that had been taken away from us. No one had stepped in, no one had helped.

"I'm a terrible agent," I muttered to myself.

"Hey, Eddie, come on, let's get something to eat, you'll feel better after that," Wreckt told me.

"Sure," I growled. We pulled up into a Burger Palace. This late, there wasn't anyone in the drive-through, and the twenty-something manning the window took our order. While we waited on the food, she chatted with Wreckt. "So, how long have you guys been together?"

I stared at her in confusion. "What do you mean?"

"It's cool," she told me, "seeing a couple guys like you, just living your best life."

"Uh…" I realized she saw the little car and two guys in it late at night and drew some conclusions. "It's not like that," I assured her. "I'm totally hetero. Him too."

"Okay, sure." She flashed me a knowing smile.

"He's an actor," I bit out. "I'm his agent."

"Oh… okay, there's no shame in that," she assured me. "Good money in gay porn."

"He's not… we're not…" I trailed off.

Arnold was laughing at me, clearly not caring what she thought.

I scowled. "Look, we just want two Burger Supremes, okay?"

"Sure thing, honey."

She couldn't bring our food fast enough for me.

Arnold pulled away after I paid with my card. I ate, hungrier than I had realized, and I felt a bit better for it.

"Okay, so you're saying you want to play good guys, the action hero. We can do that, we just need to get your career going again," I told Arnold.

He shook his head. "I want to *be* the good guy, Eddie. I want to help people. I always have. This is a second chance. I feel younger, better than ever. I think I could actually do some good now."

"What, like a soup kitchen or something?" I scoffed.

"Like kicking the asses of Russian gangsters or stopping criminals," Wreckt told me with a serious expression.

I stared at him. I really looked at him. His expression was earnest. He really thought he could do this. I wanted to tell him that only an idiot would say something like that. I couldn't do it, though. Arnold was the only one who had ever given a shit about me in probably my entire life. He was the only one who had ever stood up for me, ever.

I couldn't turn around and repay that by telling him his idea was dumb. Even if it was dumb and likely to land us in jail—or worse, the special prison set aside for those with Talents. I repressed a shudder as I thought about the rumors I had heard about the Crypt. They put the worst of the worst in there, in holes bored deep into the ground, places that never saw the light of day.

Understandably, I wanted to steer him away. "How about we finish this movie..."

I trailed off as I saw flashing lights behind us. "Aw... crap."

I shouldn't have used my card at the Burger Palace, I realized. They had probably seen the charge and pulled us up on traffic cameras or something.

He pulled over, and two SUVs pulled in behind us, with another one pulling up in front to block us off. I pulled out my "acquired" phone and brought up the camera.

"What are you doing?" Arnold asked.

"The way things went down before, I'm getting this shit on camera," I told him. I wasn't about to let them accuse me of something stupid like resisting arrest.

Several men in tactical armor piled out of the vehicles. "Arnold Wreckt, get out of the vehicle!"

They all had rifles, Ars, AKs, or some other black tactical looking things, I wasn't sure. They had FBI stenciled across their body armor.

This was bad.

Arnold climbed out of the car, hands in the air. "What seems to be the problem, officers?" He said it with his normal, friendly smile.

"Get on the ground, asshole!" one of the men bellowed. I brought the camera around on him, zooming in on his face. I might not be able to change what was happening, but I was going to document the shit out of it.

I panned back to Arnold as he knelt down. "How do you know Alexander Lloyd?" The speaker came up, weapon still leveled on Wreckt.

"I don't know who that is. Is he in Hollywood?" Wreckt looked genuinely confused. He wasn't the only one, either. I was confused as hell, too.

The talker swung the butt of his rifle into Wreckt's face. It shattered. Not Wreckt's face, the rifle butt. He had a jaw like a Greek god. I got that on camera, too.

"Would you like to try that again?" Wreckt asked in a calm voice. I recognized that voice. It was the same one he used when he told Harvey Moore to apologize right before he hit him.

"Aw, shit," I groaned to myself.

I had to intervene, or this was going to go really bad. "Look, guys, there's clearly a misunderstanding here.

"Get him out of there!" the lead FBI guy barked.

An agent opened my door and pulled me out by my shoulder. I kept the camera phone going and kept it down by my hip so they wouldn't see. "Look, if this is about the stuff with the governor and that Russian mob guy..."

"We know the governor's crooked," the FBI guy holding me snapped. "We don't care about that. We need to find Lloyd. Tell us where he's at, or we'll make your lives miserable."

"I don't know anyone named Lloyd," I told him.

One of them punched Wreckt in the side of the face, then stumbled back swearing, as he'd clearly broken his hand.

"Doesn't ring any bells," Arnold Wreckt told them.

I couldn't help but snort with laughter.

"You think this is funny?" the guy holding me snapped. He slapped me upside the head. "I can send both your pretty-boy asses to the deepest holes in the Crypt. You won't do so well there, Connors."

I had been to jail, I sure as hell didn't want to go back. "I'm telling you, neither of us know anyone named Lloyd."

"He clearly has touched the remnant," the lead FBI guy pointed at Wreckt. "Do you think we're stupid?"

I stared at him. "Do you really want me to answer that?"

The guy holding me snorted. Then, as his boss glared at him, he slapped me again.

"Tell me what I want to know, or else…"

He trailed off as several more SUVs pulled up next to us in the middle of the street. I could hear the blaring Russian rap music even before the doors opened. Guys in tracksuits carrying submachine guns piled out, and suddenly, there were guns pointed everywhere. *Man, they weren't lying, there really is a gun problem in this city.*

"Mister Karmazov has a deal with US government. We are here to take these two," a guy said. He had a spiderweb tattoo rising up his neck and across his right cheek with a disturbingly realistic spider on it. In the light from the vans, the spider coming off the spiderweb almost looked like it was crawling up his face.

"You can have them after we get what we need, not before," the FBI agent told them.

"Wait, what?" I demanded. "You're just going to turn us over to them?"

The agent who had me by the shoulder slapped me on the back of the head again. "Anton Karmazov pays his taxes and provides us information on people we want. What can you do for us?"

"We want them now, bitch," the Russian mobster snapped.

"Oh, so much for them being team players," I joked. I got slapped *again*. This was really getting old.

"Maybe they don't like paying taxes." Wreckt laughed.

"You can't *have* them right now," the FBI leader snapped. "Piss off."

The Russian snapped his fingers, and one of his guys moved over to open the car door. A gorgeous woman slid out, blonde, about six foot, in a dress that clung to her curves in a way that had my jaw dropping, and I totally forgot what we were all arguing about.

"Borislava, these men will not give us the two men we want," the Russian told her. "Retrieve them for us."

"What is she supposed to do, ask us nicely?" the FBI leader scoffed.

The Russian with the spider tattoo sneered back. "I was the one asking you nicely. This is *Bolshoy Borislava,* Big Bori, she will make you do what we want."

The FBI guys were laughing at him. She started walking forward. One of the FBI guys looked at his boss, who gave him a nod, and he pulled out a taser. "Alright, ma'am, I'm going to need you to stop right there..."

She kept coming, and he fired the taser.

She reached up and caught the electrodes where they stuck in her left breast, sparking. That forearm swelled up, along with the breast behind it. She expanded outwards, still six foot tall, but rapidly swelling, muscle and fat bulging outwards until she was nearly as broad as she was wide and stomping forward at a run.

"Oh shit," the FBI guy had time to say before she swung one massive fist at him and sent him into the lead FBI SUV hard enough to spin it out of the way, knocking several more FBI guys around like rag dolls.

The guy holding me let go and brought up his rifle, firing at her.

"Okay, I see you guys are busy, I'll just get out of the way," I told him as another FBI guy went flying.

"Arnold, get in the car!" I called.

He stood up, and he took a half-step toward Bori, as if he were ready to throw down. "Get in the *car,* man, the baddies are fighting one another, let's *go.*"

He hopped in, the shocks groaning under his weight. The little Miata coughed and sputtered as he accelerated away, and I kept the phone camera trained on the action as the Russian mobsters and FBI continued to fight it out.

"Holy crap," I told him. "Did you see that? She got, like, *huge.*"

"Her muscle tone could use some work," he noted as he drove. "She needs a personal trainer."

"She's BENT, man, maybe a Talent, you think she needs to work on that? She was throwing guys around just fine." I stopped the recording as we rounded a corner, just after she threw an FBI SUV in our general direction.

"Talent is no substitute for hard work," Arnold told me. "She could have cleaner form, too, when lifting and punching. She's likely to hurt herself."

The SUV landed on a building behind us. "One can only hope." If she hurt herself, then she wouldn't be able to hurt us.

I really hoped we didn't have to worry about the FBI guys or "Big Bori" again. Maybe we'd get lucky, and they'd all kill one another.

Somehow, as we drove away, I knew we wouldn't be that lucky.

Chapter 8

Sometime during our FBI encounter, Linus had texted me an address with an update. I noticed it almost as we were pulling up to his office.

"Crap, Linus wants us to meet him somewhere else now. He says he has a camera guy lined up," I told Wreckt.

"Do you think we should still be driving around?" Wreckt asked.

I didn't know. The FBI probably found us from me using my credit card. Granted, that wouldn't be much of a problem, I was pretty sure the Burger Palace purchase had probably been the last purchase I could afford, anyway.

If they had the little Mazda Miata tracked in their system or something, then the more we drove around in it, the more at risk we would be.

"I don't think we have a choice," I told him. I pulled up the address. "Yeah, it's halfway across town, I think we're worse off walking that far."

Arnold pulled away, the little car's engine puttering under his weight. I switched the phone's settings over to avoid the interstate, thinking it would be less likely for us to encounter law enforcement, and we drove through the back-streets of Chicago instead.

"You and Katie Rocco hit it off well." Arnold glanced over at me.

"Similar backgrounds." I didn't look over at him, and I couldn't help but slink down in the seat a bit. I liked Katie. I *really* liked her. The fact that she had recognized me after thirty years was sort of flattering. That she had signed onto the movie, too, meant she wasn't like others, that she hadn't written me and Arnold off.

"Do you think you should ask her out?" Arnold asked.

"What?" I looked over at him, fighting an edge of panic at the idea. "Arnold, we're wanted right now. You think I should try to take her on a romantic dinner somewhere? Assuming I don't get arrested or shot or something, I'm sure that would go down *swimmingly*."

"Better to try and fail than not to try at all." Arnold took another corner. We were going through some really rough parts of Chicago now, and as we pulled past obvious drug dealers, I wondered if maybe the freeway wouldn't have been a better plan.

Arnold stopped at a red light. Some guy hustled up from the corner, tapping a pistol on the driver's side window. "Yo, man, you in the wrong place. Get out the car, man."

"Drive, Arnold," I hissed.

"The light is red," Arnold told me in a patient tone. Arnold put down the window and smiled at the guy. "What seems to be the problem?"

"Get out the car, your bitch ass is going to walk," the guy told him.

"I don't think so," Wreckt said in an ominous tone.

I sighed and leaned over so he could see me. "Hey, buddy, we're having something of a rough night, could you just piss off?"

He brought his pistol up and aimed it at me. "I'm gonna put three rounds in your punk ass—"

Wreckt thumped him through the window. The little car bounced a little bit.

The would-be carjacker stumbled back and fell into a pile of garbage on the side of the street.

The light turned green, and we pulled away.

"What's it like?" I asked as we drove.

"What?" Arnold asked.

"What is it like being super strong?" I looked over at him out of the corner of my eyes. "Being able to do whatever you want."

"I can't do whatever I want." Arnold drove onward, taking the next turn. Outside, the area got a little better, then got worse as we drove past burned out cars. "There are rules."

"Only the rules you *want* to follow," I scoffed.

Arnold shook his head. "Laws exist for a reason, Eddie."

"We broke the law a few times today." I glanced at the time on my cell phone. "Or yesterday, I guess."

"We defended ourselves." Arnold shook his head.

"Like with that guy back there?" I laughed.

"The Russians as well, Eddie," Arnold told me. "This is part of being a hero, doing the right thing, protecting the innocent."

"And crippling and killing the bad guys?" I scoffed. I didn't really have much sympathy for any of them. Truthfully, I didn't have much sympathy for anyone at all. I had been a punching bag my entire life. I had never been strong. I had never had the opportunity to stand up for myself, and any time I had, things had only gotten worse for me.

"By stopping them in the most efficient manner possible so they do not have the opportunity to hurt anyone else," Arnold answered.

"That's nice in principle, but there are laws against that kind of thing as well." I gestured around outside at the torn up area we were driving through. "People like the ones out there, people like us, the laws don't work in our favor. The really bad people, the ones who accumulate money and lawyers, they make the laws work for them."

I thought about Harvey Moore and the men like him in Hollywood. I thought about the crooked politicians who had accused Arnold Wreckt and I of attacking them, when all we had been doing was trying to survive.

"The fact that some people abuse the law does not make following the law wrong," Arnold continued in a placid tone.

"Well, we'll just see how well that works out for us, huh?" I sneered. "We can compare notes on it when we're in jail or in the Crypt."

"We will clear our names, Eddie." Arnold looked over at me. "You're my agent. You'll figure it out. I have confidence in you."

"That makes one of us," I muttered. I didn't argue the point anymore, though. He had kind of turned it around on me when he said he believed in me. How was I supposed to argue with him after that?

We continued the drive in silence. I dozed off here and there, jolting awake as Arnold took sharp corners and then dozing off again.

I woke up as Arnold Wreckt pulled up to what looked like a house in a residential area. "Pull up over there." I pointed at an empty spot across the street and down a ways, just in case the FBI did have some way to track our car. Hopefully, it would buy us a few minutes to escape.

The sleep I had left my head feeling muddled. I kept replaying the day's events, the encounter with the three Russians at Norm Linus's place, the Little Tee at Norm's office, the Russian mob boss, Anton Karmazov, the politicians…

It was all a mess. I didn't know what to do about any of it. We had gotten lucky with our encounter with the FBI, where the two groups had fought one another. Otherwise, I was certain I'd be headed to be the little spoon in a federal prison or being tortured to death by the Russian mob.

As far as different fates went, I wasn't sure which one was worse.

As we went up the steps to the front door of the house, it opened. Norm Linus stood there, pistol in hand. He peered around, as if to make sure we had come alone, before he shoulder-holstered his gun. "Hey guys, any problems?"

"Nothing we couldn't handle." Wreckt smiled.

Linus gave him a nod. "Good, glad you could make it. Come on downstairs, I want you to meet Lawrence."

"Who?" I asked.

"The camera guy. He does amazing stuff, incredibly talented." Linus led the way into the house, then downstairs into the basement. The entire basement had been rigged up as a sound stage, with lighting and soundproofing.

"They call him the Spider. He runs everything through networked cameras and—"

"Quiet on the set!" a voice snapped.

"And... action," someone said.

Knowing how movie sets worked, I kept quiet, though I peered around Linus, half expecting to see some raunchy X-rated number, given that we were filming in someone's basement.

Instead, I saw two fully-dressed middle-aged men standing across a table from each other. "Alright, I'm going to go ahead and fire my squad of Star Marine Hotshooters," the one said. Then, to my bewilderment, he rolled a double handful of dice. "And... threes to hit and..." He picked up the dice and rolled them again. "Ouch, twos to wound, have you ever seen so many ones to wound?"

"You've no manner of luck, friend," the other actor told him.

Stepping closer, I saw the table had what looked like toy tanks and little action figures or something.

"Alright, I'm going to roll my saves on sixes. I'll save from your hotshooters and... ha!"

I looked between them in bewilderment as the one guy groaned and buried his face in his hands. "Four sixes? Are you kidding me, Lawrence?"

"I'm sorry, friend, them's the breaks. Very well played, just bad luck there at the end. Good game, my friend." Lawrence shook the other man's hand and then he said, "Cut!"

"I really thought I had you that time." The other guy shook his head.

"Me too. It's a dice game. Hey, I've got to meet with these guys, give me a few, okay?" Lawrence had a British accent, which I found weird. We were in Chicago. What was a Brit doing here?

His friend gave a nod. "Yeah, sure thing."

Lawrence came over. "Linus, are these the guys?"

"Yep." Linus nodded. "And Clarence over there has the script."

"Yo, dawg." Clarence came over from where he had been seated, watching… well, watching whatever these two had been doing. Some kind of game, I supposed. I had never imagined someone would watch other people playing some kind of game.

"Clarence here has a fantastic script, just needs a little work on the dialog, pacing, plot, historical accuracy, characterization, theme, story, and grammar. Shouldn't take more than three or four rewrites to get something workable." Linus nodded. "In the meantime, we can start shooting right away on this action number that Miss Rocco told me about."

"Action number…" I stared at him, not understanding what he meant.

"Yeah, the bodybuilder and his personal trainer who run afoul of the Russian mob, those pinko-commie former-KGB fucks. Sounds like a good one to build some crowd appeal while we're working on the period piece."

"Yo, Russian mobsters?" Clarence asked. "That sounds dope. Those guys are assholes."

"We don't really have a script," I protested. I looked at Arnold in a panic. This wasn't a script or a story, this was real life.

"Show him the video you took." Wreckt pointed at my phone.

"Oh, you've got some test footage?" Lawrence came forward and held out his hand.

"It's not really professional quality." I hesitantly held up my phone. He took it before I could protest any further.

"That's fine." He tapped on the screen, flipping through options faster than I could register, and then waved at a big television screen. "Here we go."

The clip started playing there. I hadn't known that was possible.

"These camera phones really have incredible quality," Linus noted as they watched the clip. "Oh, I like that part there, showing the corruption of the FBI. This is good stuff."

"Uh, it's sort of a documentary." I looked down at the ground, feeling weirdly embarrassed at the praise.

"Even better." Lawrence nodded. "We can rig up some drones with cameras, follow you all. I've already seen the alerts the governor put out. You can't buy better marketing."

"Really?" I looked up in surprise. My experiences with being wanted and arrested before had been all to the negative. I'd lost pretty much everything, and Harvey Moore's lawyers had used my arrest as a further way to discredit my accusations against him.

"Everyone is going to know your names." Linus nodded. "Instant stardom for Arnold Wreckt, assuming the CIA, NSA, FBI, or the ATF don't put a black bag over his head and stick him in the deepest hole at the bottom of the Crypt." He looked at me. "Oh, you, too."

"So, uh, how do we avoid that?" I swallowed in fear.

"The footage is amateurish, but it has a sort of charm to it." Lawrence waved a hand. "We need more to tell the whole story. More of this, we can splice it all together, fill in the blanks. Though there is a sort of *in media res* feeling to it, we probably can lead in with some of the news footage…"

"I like it." Arnold nodded. "We can fight these bastards and show everyone that we're the good guys."

"*We* aren't anything," I protested. "I'm just your agent." I couldn't help but think "accomplice to murder" and "conspiracy to commit crimes" would come up if I got too eager about helping to go after anyone.

"The wanted notices are for both of you." Linus adjusted his glasses as he looked over at me. "Really, it makes far better marketing appeal with a sort of Butch Cassidy and the Sundance Kid sort of appeal." He waved at Arnold and I, as if we were an obvious match.

"Uh, I'm fuzzy on the historical details, but in the movie, they died in Bolivia, right?" I asked.

"Yeah, such a great movie. Too bad Redman's politics are as red as his hair." Linus nodded. "They got massacred by the entire Bolivian Army, blaze of glory, really defining moment in cinema."

"Strangely, that doesn't appeal." I rolled my eyes.

"I have a question. Would it be possible to get those guys in the movie?" Wreckt asked.

"Okay, no, we are not seeing if the Bolivian Army is booked," I snapped at him. "I, for one, am not going out in a blaze of glory, or any other blaze, for that matter."

"There is always Bonnie and Clyde," Wreckt offered. "That was a story that is very big here in the United States."

"Um, in the first case against that, they were romantically engaged, dude, and like I told the woman at Burger Palace, I'm strictly *hetero*," I growled. "In the second, just in case the first isn't enough, they *still* died, they got, like, machine-gunned by, like, Texas Rangers, so again, no thank you."

"Hmm, Bonnie and Clyde are more of a Greek Tragedy anyway, sort of semi-operatic." Linus nodded. "Doomed lovers whose faults lead to their untimely deaths. You know... if you both were willing to go shirtless…"

"I have no issues with that." Wreckt started taking off his shirt.

I waved a hand in a futile attempt to stop him. "He doesn't mean right now."

I turned back to Linus. "And *no*, I am not doing anything shirtless. Look, can we please focus? Assuming we do this whole documentary thing, how does that clear our names?"

"We do it live streaming"—Lawrence spread his hands—"across BlueTube, Spasm, all the streaming services. I monitor the chat and comments, pass messages to you both, we use that to crowdfund the period piece."

"I think I only understood like one word in three there." I shook my head.

"Okay, so we focus everything on the big guy." Linus waved at Wreckt. "You"—he pointed at me—"will carry a phone recording with you pretty much all the time, and Lawrence will manage the streams."

"I'm thinking a subscriber-only all-access, some teasers and highlights for everyone else." Lawrence nodded. "Mega-chats get direct responses and actions."

"Mega-whats?" I asked.

"When they tip us, we respond with a thank you. Sometimes, you can really get a crowd fired up, start bidding wars, that kind of thing," Lawrence told me. "With gaming or something, you might do something crazy, like if they hit five hundred, you try to solo a boss with a crap weapon or something like that."

"I could hit people just with my left hand," Arnold offered. "Or try to juggle while I fight them!"

"Yeah, we'll work on the reward tiers." Lawrence shook his head. "Anyway, this will send your story out live, where the FBI, NSA, and CIA can't make it disappear. We can develop enough of a personal interest side to keep people watching and enough action to get them started."

Lawrence went over to a computer and pulled up a dozen websites, hopping from one to the next faster than I could follow. "Alright, so I've registered Get Wreckt, LLC, set you up streaming accounts on the major live streaming services, and since I've got a premium account, I've already got you monetized. I'm putting up your clip here as a trailer along with the wanted clips. Let's go ahead and shoot introductory shots."

He picked up a camera and brought it around, lights pointing at Wreckt. "So, be as natural as possible and just say who you are and why you're doing this… and *action*."

"Hey there." Wreckt smiled for the camera. "I'm Arnold Wreckt. Some really bad people are trying to kill me, some other bad people have accused me of crimes I didn't commit. I'm going to be coming to you live, while I clear my name. For the people after me… you better watch out or… you'll get Wreckt." He pointed at the screen, and Lawrence gave a nod. "Cut. Very nice, very natural. I like it."

He turned the camera on me. Suddenly, I had lights in my eyes, and I could barely see. "Same thing, bud, ready, and *action*."

Every single thought went out of my head. I hadn't been in front of a camera in thirty years. I opened my mouth to speak, froze up, stared at the camera, closed my mouth, opened it again, and finally mumbled, "I'm Eddie Connor. I used to be a child actor, now I'm an agent. Don't do drugs, kids."

"Cut." Lawrence shook his head. "We need to work on that one."

"I'm not going to be in front of the camera. I don't need an intro," I snapped.

"Right, the mysterious man behind the camera angle, dawg, I like it," Clarence told me. "Build up the anticipation for your reveal."

"Better yet, *no* reveal," I snapped. "I really don't like this. It feels like some kind of reality TV gimmick." No matter how desperate things had gotten for Arnold and I, I had managed to keep us out of the horrors of reality television, at least.

"Oh, I like that." Linus pointed his finger at me. "We could go the whole angle, two failed actors trying to make the cut and get a second chance at stardom. It will pull the human interest side of things, especially with your past, Connors."

"The fuck it will." I rounded on him. "I'm not an actor. This isn't about me. I'm not in this, got it?" I didn't want an acting career, I sure as hell didn't want any of this being a hero piece that Arnold Wreckt was after. I wanted to take care of him as his agent. I wanted to get through this alive and hopefully suffering as little relative pain as possible in the process.

Lawrence went on, "I've transferred everything from your phone over to this one. It's a top-end phone. You'll have plenty of battery life." He went over and pulled some more gear out and worked on it for a moment before coming back to us. "There we are, I set up some low-profile ear buds so you both will be able to hear me back here in the command center. When we start getting mega-chats or lots of subscribes, I'll let you all know so you can properly react."

He came over and handed each of us earbuds. They were small and flesh colored, so it would be hard to notice that we even had them in.

"Those don't have any real range themselves, they only work based off the cell phone signal or if my drones are in the area, so don't lose the phone," Lawrence told us.

"Nice." Wreckt nodded as he jammed it in his ear. "Can you hear us?"

"We're standing right here, dude." I put my hands over my face in embarrassment.

"I'll be watching through the stream," Lawrence told us. "I'll also be checking our projected earnings against what we need for the film."

"This is dumb," I muttered to myself as I took the earpiece.

"Did George Washington say this was dumb as he crossed the Delaware to kill the British on Christmas?" Linus snapped. "Did Rudy Valentino say this was dumb when he got his first big hit?"

"Wasn't he in silent film?" Wreckt frowned. "It would be hard to hear what he said."

"That doesn't matter," Linus barked. "What matters is this is our best opportunity to get this film off the ground. We crowdfund it, we get the money we need for props and sets and other actors, and then we show those commie Hollywood *fucks* what a good movie is."

"Hopefully, we clear our names and don't end up in the Crypt," I muttered. "Fine, what's our first step?" I was resigned to it all at this point. Linus and Lawrence had railroaded us along. There was nothing to do but go along with it and hope we didn't die.

"We need something big to launch your channel," Lawrence told me. "That clip on your phone is a nice little teaser, but we need something really huge."

"I have just the idea," Katie Rocco spoke from behind us. I had been so focused on the conversation that I hadn't even heard her come in.

"What's that?" I asked, my mouth going dry as I saw her dressed in a tight-fitting jumpsuit. I wondered how long she had been watching us. I wondered if maybe I shouldn't have taken my shirt off after all. Not that I had much to show. Standing next to Arnold Wreckt with no shirt, I would probably look like a five-year-old next to his father.

Katie came over, tapping the television screen still frozen on the big Russian woman throwing the SUV. "The guys after you, they fought each other, right?"

"How'd you know?" I asked.

"I watched the video. It's already up." Katie smiled at me. "Over three hundred comments so far. You're starting to trend. Anyway, get them to come to you and then get them fighting each other. The absolute best would be if they reveal that they know you're innocent, or at least prove themselves guilty."

I considered that. "We'd have to be there in the middle of it. They will probably both be trying to kill us or arrest us or just hurt us really bad."

"Of course." Katie smiled. "I didn't say it would be easy, but you're trying to clear your client's name, right? You're supposed to be a good agent. Good agents look out for their clients, no matter how hard things get."

I gave her a glower. "You read that on my website." I didn't have much heat to that glare though. I was more excited that she *had* checked out my website. She was interested in me. No one had been interested in me since…

I wiped that thought out of my head and focused on the task at hand. "Alright, we go to this place, we get all the baddies there, we get them fighting one another, and hopefully, they incriminate themselves on live television—"

“Live stream,” Lawrence corrected. “No one watches television anymore, least of all live.”

“…we get a million or so views, and then we make Arnold Wreckt a movie star,” I finished.

“What could go wrong?” Arnold smiled.

“Great, you just had to ask that question.” I glowered at him. He didn’t seem to care.

“We need someplace out of the way, someplace people won’t get hurt when things get violent.” I looked around at the others, my brain blanking on where we could go in Chicago for that sort of thing.

“I got just the place,” Clarence spoke up. “Little Tee, he has a dope grow facility in these abandoned factories on the South Side… Uh, we aren’t filming right now, are we?”

“No, not right now,” Lawrence assured him.

“Oh, good, he would probably bust a cap in my ass if he knew it was me that told anyone. Anyway, that whole part of town, there’s nothing there, like twenty blocks of empty factories and people with meth labs and illegal dope grows.”

“That could work.” I looked over at Arnold. “What do you think?”

He flexed his arm, looking thoughtfully at the fist he made. “Do you think she will be there?”

"Who?" I asked.

"The big woman," Arnold said. "Borislava."

"I am almost certain that she'll show up." I frowned. "I mean, she was muscle for the Russians before, why wouldn't she be there now?"

"I'm in." Wreckt smiled. "They are going to get Wreckt."

I scowled at him. "Dammit, man, save those lines for the camera!"

Chapter 9

"How are we going to do this?" Wreckt asked as we drove away from our meetup with Linus and the others.

"I figured I would turn the camera on, start streaming, and then we could just taunt them into showing up?"

He considered that as he drove. Katie Rocco had offered to come along with, but at least so far, she wasn't wanted by anyone, so I would rather she stay safe and out of all this, so I had politely declined the offer.

She had also told us not to worry if anything happened to the little red Miata. Seeing as she had a successful acting career for the past forty-odd years and I hadn't, I had to assume she didn't really care what happened to the car.

Frankly, I wasn't sure why she was helping us at all. Maybe she just found it amusing.

I certainly wouldn't have helped us under similar circumstances. These Russian mobsters were psycho, and I didn't even know what to think about the government types after us.

Wreckt drove the little red car like he had stolen it, weaving in and out of traffic with disregard for traffic signals and road rules. It was well past midnight, though, so the streets were mostly empty.

"Hey, I'm bringing us live. This driving is actually pretty good as a teaser," Lawrence called in my ear. "Move the camera around and get video of him driving, would you?"

"Yeah, sure," I muttered. I held up the phone, looking at Wreckt. "What's happening?" I asked.

Wreckt looked over, seeming to realize it was time to put on his game face. "The Russian mob is after us. We're going someplace where we can face them and not put anyone in danger." He downshifted and took a corner while looking at the camera, and as the tires squealed and we swept dangerously past a brick wall of a closed and boarded up business, I felt my stomach tense up.

"It is always important to face the things you fear, to take them head on, rather than to run away," Wreckt told the audience.

"Nice," Lawrence said in our earbuds. "Go a bit more of the human element, maybe some background?"

"When I was younger, growing up in Europe, there was a bully on my street. He used to call me names, and he once slapped me. I was too afraid to do anything. My father, he took me to the side, and he told me that I needed to be strong so that I would not be afraid. That day, I started training, four hours every day at the gym. Hard work and confidence paid off. My bully never bothered me again."

He finished up as we swerved off the road into an abandoned parking lot. This was the area that Clarence had told us about.

"To the Russian mobsters who want to kill me, here I am," Wreckt told the audience.

I panned around the area so they would see where we were and zoomed in on the street sign and then the front of the building, then went back to Wreckt.

We needed more than that, though. We needed those FBI guys here. I added for good measure, "Yeah, and you dudes looking for Lloyd, he's here, too. You better show up with all your goodies."

Wreckt raised an eyebrow at me, and I shrugged. I still had no idea who this guy they wanted was. Maybe he worked with the Russians or something. Either way, I didn't care.

"We will be waiting for you inside," Wreckt told them. "Let us see how brave you are in a fair fight."

"And cutting audio while you go inside, try to do a pan around the interior of the building for mood setting. I'm putting in some rock music to keep them interested." Lawrence's voice was relaxed in our earbuds as he talked. "Our views jumped by about four thousand, good job, guys."

"Four thousand is good?" I panned the phone's camera around as we came into the building.

"Four thousand is great, especially when it's organic growth like this. People are really eating the bully angle. Oh, hey, we just got our first superchat. It's from some guy named TrouserSnek. He just tipped us five bucks and said no way that Lloyd is in Chicago this time of year."

"Oh, this guy knows who he is?" I asked.

"Hold on, chat is going nuts. Oh, another superchat, twenty dollars from some guy in Buenos Aires. He said he loves the guerrilla-style shooting, but the lighting needs work."

"It's an abandoned building, what are we supposed to do about it?" I didn't know what to think about the whole live thing. There was bound to be a hundred armchair generals in their parents' basements, telling us how much we sucked and how they would do things better.

"Oh, here we go, a lot of chats talking about the wanted ads. Oh, the governor of Illinois just got on. He's telling us we should surrender ourselves, and we have about four hundred people telling him to shut his face." Lawrence laughed. "Oh, this one is good, someone just tipped us forty bucks to tell the governor to stuff it."

"Shit, I'll do that for free, put me on audio," I said on impulse. I turned the camera to face me. "Hey, you fat jerk, I saw you and your little goblin buddy taking bribes from the Russian mob. That's why you want us arrested. You also stepped on my dick trying to run away. So shut your pie-hole or come down here yourself, okay?"

"Easy on the language, you don't want us to get demonetized," Lawrence cautioned me. "You're back on mute. That was pretty good, a little rough. Maybe practice the insults a little. And do you mean he stepped on his dick?"

"No, he literally stepped on mine trying to escape." I kicked a piece of debris out of my way. "It really hurt. Dude has to be three hundred pounds. Uh, we're going to throw down with these guys, will the violence be a problem?" I asked. I wasn't even sure what "demonetized" meant, but if cursing was a problem...

"Nah, we'll be fine, BlueTube knows that this stuff sells. We'll put in a violence disclaimer, which just means more people will tune in. Oh, gotta go, someone is trying to hack the feed."

I wasn't even sure what that meant. I kept panning the camera around as Wreckt and I walked toward the center of the warehouse.

As we got near an area with a generator and lights, I saw the signs of the marijuana grow house that Clarence had told us about. There were security cameras up there too, and Wreckt waved at them.

"Putting you guys back up on audio while I handle this other thing. Feel free to talk. People like banter," Lawrence told us.

"I wonder what they made here before?" Wreckt bent over to look at a big rusting gear that wasn't connected to anything anymore.

"I dunno, I know about as much about factories and industry as I do about women," I joked. Actually, come to think of it, it wasn't much of a joke. I didn't know much about either. I'd never had an honest job in my life, unless you counted the few times I had bused tables to keep a roof over our heads.

He toed a pile of rusting machinery. "My father worked in a steel mill when I was a child. The mill closed when I was a teenager, and many people were out of work. The government said the mill was bad for the ground, bad for the air, bad for the people that worked there. It was very hard for the town without the mill, and many people had to move away to find work, or else they gave up."

He looked at the camera. "It saddens me to see things that were once places of work and craft to be abandoned."

That was a lot deeper than I had expected from him.

Not knowing what else to say, I said, "This spot is as good as any to wait for them."

"Do you think she will show up?" Wreckt asked.

"Yeah, I'm sure the Russians will be here," I assured him. I wasn't sure why he said "she" and not "they." Maybe he was worried about their big woman. She sure scared *me*.

On cue, out the doors of the building, I saw car lights as vehicles rolled up, and I heard shouts in what I assumed was Russian. I put the camera over on them and moved a bit back so I could show Wreckt in the shot and also be a little safer behind him.

A moment later, I heard a *thud-thud-thud* as a helicopter swung by overhead, spotlights going through the side windows of the industrial building. More vehicles rolled up on that side of the building. I heard shouted commands as men jumped out of vehicles.

I had not expected the response to come so quickly. I panned the camera one way and then the other as the two groups advanced.

"Uh, do you think they're going to talk?" I asked in a low voice.

"They are not here to talk," Wreckt answered. "They are here to get Wreckt."

Coming through the front doors at the lead was a team of Russians in their ever-present fitness suits and armed with AKs. *I really need to learn what the different weapons are called.*

Really, I was vague on all the details. My father had a few hunting rifles, but other than knowing a bullet went in one end and out the other, I didn't really know much about them.

Behind the lead Russians came the same mid-level guy who had started the attack with the FBI guys earlier. In the crazy lighting, the spider tattoo on his face seemed to crawl and move in a disturbing fashion. Walking behind him was the six-foot beautiful blonde who could turn into some kind of bulky terror.

"Okay, guys," I told them, "I am glad you all could make it. I think we got off on the wrong foot…"

"We are going to kill you," the mid-level thug told us, "chop your dangly bits off, and mail them to your family."

"My parents might be down for that. I think my insurance policy hasn't run out yet, so that would pay out pretty well for them," I answered. "Oh, hey, here come mystery guests number two."

A dozen or so figures in black tactical armor moved in from the side doors. I was expecting more FBI types, but none of them had that standard yellow FBI text on their armor, nor did they have any markings. They wore black face masks, too, the kind people wore when they robbed a bank or did something similarly bad and didn't want their identity known. I found that worrisome.

I smiled. "So, are you all here?"

"Down on the ground, Lloyd, or we open fire!" one of them shouted.

"I'm not this Lloyd guy, clearly," I told them. "Arnold, would you care to explain?"

I panned the camera over to him, even as I caught a glint up near the ceiling, and I spotted a couple of Lawrence's drones—at least, I assumed they were his—come in through holes in the roof. They had cameras trained on everyone, so hopefully, this stream was going out.

"I want to clear our names," Arnold told them. "The Russian mob attacked us without warning. They were there to bribe the governor and mayor to clear out businesses so their boss could take over areas of the city."

"I'm doing an identity match on these guys," Lawrence spoke in my ear. "Based off their faces and what I can find in the system, the leader of these Russians is Sergei. He works for Anton Karmazov. No idea on the guys in black. Did you lot piss someone else off?"

"Shut up, you," Sergei said at the same time.

"Our feed is trending up again, try to get them to say something incriminating," Lawrence suggested in a helpful fashion.

"Sergei, you just say what Karmazov tells you to do, so how about you call him down here, and we can straighten this out?" Wreckt called.

The Russians and the black ops team had weapons trained on each other and us. I wasn't sure what the guns would do to Wreckt, but I knew they would put holes in me. Sure, I *probably* would heal from those holes, but that didn't mean they wouldn't hurt.

"Lloyd, this is the last time I'm going to tell you!" The speaker was the black ops leader, I guessed. "Get down on the ground, or this is going to get really, really painful. We know you're not Eddie Connors, just like we know it wasn't Kurt Russel at the airport."

"Of *course* I'm Eddie Connors," I snapped at him. "Who the hell else would I be?"

"A ninety-year-old shapechanger who looks like a fifteen-year-old failed child actor," the black ops guy told me. Unlike the others, he wasn't wearing a face mask, and his handsome face wore a confident smirk. "Eddie Connors is forty-five. We're not stupid."

"Ohhhh… that's not good," Lawrence told us, his British accent clipped. "I just figured out who they think you are. This guy called Alexander Lloyd, he's like on every top ten most wanted list, not just here in the US, like every single one in the entire world. This dude is seriously bad business… but his name just spiked our viewers. We just broke a hundred thousand views."

I didn't have time to process that. I focused on the talker and spoke, "Look, I look sixteen, thank you, because I'm BENT, you morons. That's in my police record, which *should* have been sealed." I scowled. This was getting to be too much about me, and it was all live. "Look, I don't know who this Alexander Lloyd guy is, but it sure as hell isn't me."

"I didn't say *Alexander* Lloyd," the team leader said in a dangerous voice. "It's him, take him down!"

My eyes went wide. "Hey, guys, let's talk about this—"

They opened fire on us before I could finish.

I dove to the side, hiding behind rusting machinery as bullets smashed into everything around me.

"Hey, camera guy, back on target!" Lawrence barked in my ear. "We don't get paid for this if all they see is the ground. My drones have a top down right now, but we need some up close action."

"The things I do for my clients," I muttered as I held the phone up over the edge.

"We need a better angle, are you even looking at the screen?" Lawrence sounded exasperated.

I muttered some choice words under my breath and popped my head up, bringing the camera around to try and get some good video.

Wreckt had gone for cover in the grow lab behind a big industrial freezer, and as I centered the camera on him, he turned around and grabbed the large appliance. "I think you all need to chill out."

He picked it up and threw it. I managed to keep the camera on target as it plowed through black ops guys and Russians, right up until it slammed into the big Russian woman, who started bulking up. "Oh, crap."

She kicked the freezer out of her way, one smooth, slender leg swelling out into a huge limb.

The blow flung the industrial freezer into another group of the black ops guys, sending them flying like bowling pins.

Russians were shooting at them and at us. A bullet whipped past my ear close enough that I felt the wind of its passage. I dropped back down, then peeked around the edge of the machinery, camera out.

"Bori, focus on the big guy," Sergei ordered her. "We will handle the others."

One of the black ops guys had some kind of big cannon thing, and he angled it around and fired it at her. It was a net launcher, and it draped the net over her and triggered an electrical outburst. She reached through the net, caught the cable leading back to the launcher, and pulled hard. Her attacker flew toward her, and she punted him up through the roof.

"Arnold, your friend seems angry!" I called out to him.

Wreckt moved forward to meet her, and she bent to grab a fallen I-beam.

"Wait!" Wreckt called to her. "You are lifting that wrong! Your back should be straight; you could injure yourself lifting like that. Center your shoulders over your hips."

"Like this?" Bori adjusted her stance.

"Yes, that is much better," Arnold told her, even as bullets bounced off his back and shoulders.

"Thanks," Bori told him. Then, before I could shout a warning, she picked up the I-beam and swung it like an oversized baseball bat right into his chest.

Wreckt went flying overhead and smashed through the back wall of the building.

"That's not good," I muttered to myself. I started running in that direction, but a black ops goon stepped out in front of me. "I found him, I found Lloyd!"

He brought his weapon up, and I dodged the other way as he fired. I wasn't sure what he carried, and I didn't want to know.

"Good dodge," Lawrence told me. "Oh, hey, we got a mega-chat. Someone wants you to kick the black ops team leader in the nuts."

I panted as I ran, dodging around a corner. "How the hell am I supposed to—"

I ran into the team leader and two of his guys. I did the first thing that came to mind and kicked him in the nads. His buddy promptly shot me with a shotgun, point blank.

"Ow, ow, ow," I gasped, dropping down and feeling at the hole he'd torn through my stomach. "You shot me, you prick."

"He's down, Lloyd's down!" The guy shouted.

Bori stepped up behind him. "You are up." She kicked him from behind, her massive leg going up between his legs and launching him up through the roof.

"Oh, shit," I groaned. I backed away, not even bleeding anymore as my stomach knitted itself back together. "Hey, uh, Bori, we can talk this out, right?"

The team leader, having recovered from my nut-shot, turned and fired into her. I was close enough to see the bullets impacting the layers of fat and muscle tissue and bouncing out, her entire body jiggling like gelatin. One of the bullets bounced off her and smashed into my shoulder hard enough to knock me back.

She backhanded him, and he went flying over my head, smashing into something heavy with an ominous crunch.

Bori stalked toward me. "Sorry, kid, the boss wants you dead, and he has me over a barrel."

"Look, maybe we can work something out?" I asked her.

She hesitated, raising one huge foot to bring it down on me. "Can you save my family from him?"

"I don't think so," I admitted.

"Ah, mate, you should have said yes," Lawrence called in my ear.

"Sorry, then." Bori started to bring her foot down to smash me into paste.

Wreckt came in from the side, slamming into her and sending her tumbling and rolling. "You need to keep your mass centered," he called out to her as she rolled through a group of Russians. "Keep a low center of gravity!"

"Stop helping her," I hissed at him as I got to my feet.

"I can't help it, she has a lot of potential." Wreckt backhanded a goon who tried to come up behind him.

"Oh, got a mega-chat from Massive Tool. He wants Wreckt to ask her on a date," Lawrence told us.

Wreckt shrugged. "Borislava, if you aren't busy tomorrow night, would you like to go on a date? We can talk fitness pointers."

She hurled a huge electric motor at us.

I dodged. Arnold took it, and he went tumbling with it as it smashed him through the back wall of the building once more.

That left me looking at her as she came at me, and I did the smart thing and ran.

Chapter 10

The unfortunate thing about running away is you often run into other things.

I hadn't gone ten feet before I ran into a pair of the black ops goons. They opened fire on me, and I let out a scream as bullets tore into me. I managed to tumble out of their line of fire, crawling across the ground.

"Target located!" one of them shouted.

I rolled onto my back, scooting on my butt as I brought the camera around. I might be about to die, but I was going to make sure no one complained that I hadn't done my job as Arnold Wreckt's agent.

The two goons came around the corner, bringing their weapons up. Borislava stepped in behind them.

"Uh, guys, fair warning, you might want to look behind you," I told them.

"Screw you, we're not that dumb," the lead one said as he leveled the weapon on my face.

"Your funeral," I muttered.

Borislava kicked that one, and he gave a perfect Wilhelm scream as he went flying. The other one turned fast and fired into Borislava, but the bullets just bounced off her. She reached out and caught him by the barrel of his rifle and swung him like a hammer-throw.

He would have made a distance record for sure if he hadn't slammed into a metal I-beam.

"Nice throw," I gasped at her. I was pretty sure they'd shot me in my kidneys. The agony was incredible. She turned toward me, her head lowering, her eyes narrowing.

"Look," I told her, "you're clearly very talented, too talented to be working for those goons." I reached into a pocket and pulled out a business card. The first one was spattered with my blood, and I threw it away and pulled out another one as I got to my feet. "Here, I'm a talent agent. We're making a movie. I bet I could land you a role."

She stepped forward and reached out and took the card, her two huge fingers bigger than my entire hand. Borislava peered at the text on my card and looked at me in turn.

I smiled at her. "I only take a 15 percent cut, and only if you get paid—"

She hit me.

I tumbled end over end. My legs slammed into something, and I felt the bones shatter. I struck a wall and flopped to the floor, every bone in my body broken, and I lay there, my arms and legs flopping uselessly. I tried to scream, but all my bones were broken, and my diaphragm seemed paralyzed.

"Oh, that looked painful," Lawrence spoke in my ear. "I got a great shot of it though, and I've spliced that with your phone camera. Good job holding onto it, by the way."

I was in complete and total agony. I wanted to sob and scream, but all I could manage was a wet groan. I couldn't even pass out. My bones were knitting themselves back together, jerking themselves back into position, and I howled in agony as all of my ribs straightened themselves, one after the other, cracking back into place like a series of fireworks.

Two Russian goons came over, and they stared at me in horror as my body reassembled itself. "What the hell *are* you?" one of them asked.

My spine jolted itself back into place, vertebrae slotting back in even as my central nervous system reconnected. I talked around a broken jaw, "Just another poor BENT bastard." I slurred the words like I was drunk.

"Target is over here," a voice shouted. "He's shifting! We need to take him down!"

I looked behind me, dropping my head back and flopping my still-broken arm around so the audience would get to watch, too. That hurt enough to draw a whimper, even as the bones started to pop back into place.

Another team of black ops goons had come up from the other direction, weapons out and aimed at me.

"Oh for God's sake…"

"Hey, assholes, get away from my boyfriend!" a voice shouted.

All of us looked over. Striding through the hole that Wreckt had made in the back wall came Katie Rocco. She wore the same tight black jumpsuit and a pair of tall boots. She had a flamethrower on her back, and she kicked it on, the blue pilot flame glowing.

"Did she just call me her boyfriend?" I asked in a shocked tone.

She cut loose with the flamethrower. I hated fire, and I got as low as I could as she swept it into the black ops goons, then into the Russians on the other side of me. I hugged the ground, all the thoughts frightened out of my head by the horrific heat. I heard screaming. I wasn't sure if it was me or the guys she'd roasted.

I heard her boot steps as she came up next to me. "Time to go, Eddie."

My legs had mostly put themselves back into place, and I stumbled to my feet. She sent more spurts of flame across the building. I didn't wait around to see the results; I limped out the way she had entered, only turning around when I was clear of the building. I trained the camera that direction as well, still unsteady on my feet.

I wouldn't have thought there was enough in the place to burn properly, but the whole place seemed to have caught fire. She strode out of it, her black hair tossing in the heat and wind of the flames, her face alight and shining.

Wreckt came up. "She knows how to make an entrance."

"Yeah," I said in a low voice. "An exit, too."

She walked up to us. "I think we're done here, right?"

As the roof of the building collapsed and flames roared up into the night sky, I couldn't help but agree.

Lawrence had cut our feed. We rode back in Katie's huge Mercedes SUV.

"How many vehicles do you have?" I asked.

"A few," was all she answered.

"This is a good vehicle," Wreckt commented as he climbed into the back seat. "Excellent machining, nicely fitted out, plenty of space in the back seat."

"Thank you, Arnold," Katie told him. "It's the AMG G63. I got it with all the upgrades, over five hundred horsepower, full connectivity, luxury seats. It's the same model one of the Saudi princes drives."

I wanted desperately to ask her what she meant when she had stepped in and rescued me. Seated next to her in the luxury SUV's front passenger seat, I couldn't manage to even open my mouth to say the words.

"Alright, guys, fantastic work," Lawrence spoke in my earbud.

"Thank you, Lawrence," Katie said sweetly. "Wonderful job getting me here, as well; my navigation system was struggling with the address."

"You can hear him, too?" Wreckt asked from the back seat.

She tapped one ear. "I made him give me an earbud, too."

"Our viewers spiked amazingly on your entrance, Miss Rocco," Lawrence reported. "All in all, great success on our first live stream. Our number of subscribers is really high as well. The stream is also trending on Dribble, it's been dribbed over four hundred thousand times."

"Uh, we burned the building down," I had to mention. "Isn't that a felony?"

"Self-defense," Katie told me with a straight face.

"We didn't get anything to clear our names." I hiked a thumb at Wreckt and then back at me. That hurt. Actually, my whole body hurt. "He got slammed through a wall," I felt the need to remind them.

"Twice," Wreckt boasted with a broad smile that was all perfect white, even teeth. "Bori is a very strong and capable woman."

"I got shot multiple times and had just about every bone in my body broken," I growled. "Those black ops guys thought I was this most wanted dude and kept shooting me…"

Katie flashed me a smile. "Hey, you're alive, isn't that good enough?"

I couldn't scowl at her. I couldn't manage it. She was too pretty and too cheerful.

"With how this is looking, we could get corporate sponsors," Lawrence went on. "I'm already getting business queries for brand placement. Eddie, you should check your site as well. You are bound to have picked up some traffic. Linus says he already has some film financiers lined up."

I brought up my business email account on my phone and blinked. "I have over a hundred emails."

I sorted through them as Katie drove. There were forty or fifty people wanting me to represent them, with full applications and everything. There were another twenty or thirty people reaching out regarding casting Wreckt, and even a few to cast *me*. That was a serious shock, as I'd been toxic in Hollywood ever since *Roboslayer Three* had imploded.

There were three marriage proposals for Arnold Wreckt, two for me, and another two for Katie Rocco.

I looked over at her, finally feeling calm enough to ask the question that had been hanging in the air. I said in a quiet voice, "You, uh, called me your boyfriend. That was just for the cameras… right?"

She reached over while driving, caught me by the front of my shirt, and pulled me in for a kiss.

I enjoyed it, but I also didn't want us in a crash. "Eyes on the road, eyes on the road!"

She sighed and let me go. "Eddie, you need to lighten up."

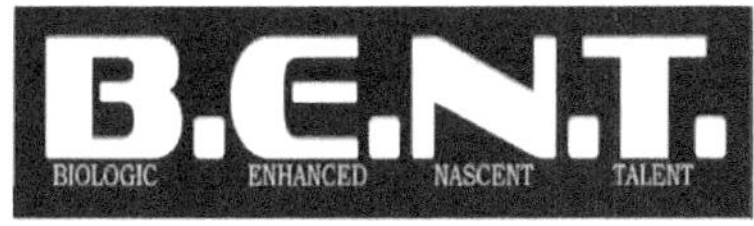

We regrouped at Linus's office.

"Great job, guys," Linus told us. "Wreckt is back in a big way, and there's a ton of interest in the period piece as well as this action flick."

"I thought we were live streaming it," I asked in confusion.

"We are, but we can make a movie out of it after we live stream it. Sort of like a twofer," Lawrence told us. "The live stream can act as a teaser and marketing for a full movie."

"This gets the investors into it." Linus nodded. "They bring a lot of money to the table."

"Great, money is good." I nodded.

"Money isn't everything, right?" Katie arched an eyebrow.

I stared at her like a deer in the headlights.

Wreckt elbowed me, and I coughed. "Yeah, uh, there are things more important than money."

"Anyway," Linus went on, "we can meet these investors tomorrow— Well, I guess it is later today, at this point. I'll need Clarence and Eddie to talk the scripts for their movies."

"I don't *have* a script," I protested.

"You *are* the script." Linus glowered at me. "Just tell them what's happened and the setup. Maybe some hints of an ending."

"I don't know how this is going to end," I protested. "We're not in a movie, this is real life. They're really trying to kill us."

"Then sprinkle in a few hints about a big explosive ending, some kind of face-off, the plucky sidekick bites the bullet, and that gives the hero the motivation to win, something like that." Linus shrugged. "It's just a script. Most of the time, the actors don't even read it."

Katie yawned. "I prefer to make it up as I go anyway."

"Exactly." Linus pointed at her. "Be like Katie: make some stuff up and go with it."

"Plucky sidekick dying…" I frowned. "Hey, wait, if Arnold is the big hero, who would the sidekick be?"

They stared at me. Katie giggled a bit.

"No, no way," I protested. "I am not the sidekick. I'm a joint protagonist. If I'm in this… this… movie, I'm credited just as much as anyone!"

"If a man represents himself, he has a fool for a client." Linus smirked.

"Oh, shut up," I growled.

"Two p.m., meet back here," Linus told us. "Wreckt, until then, you probably better lay low. No more run-ins, we don't want to scare off our investors."

"I've got a place they can stay," Katie assured him.

"Those black ops guys, do we know who they are? They might have some kind of federal connection," I had to bring that up.

"Yeah, they're NSA, CIA, or some other alphabet soup," Linus growled. "Bunch of jack-booted fascists. They've been running abductions of impoverished BENT, I think for experimentation. I tried doing a documentary on it, but I couldn't get anywhere."

I didn't know about that. Some of Norm Linus's rants and theories were really out there. I looked at the others. "Are we not worried about them tracking us? You know, bank accounts, cell phones, that sort of thing?"

"I paid someone to mask all our gear," Lawrence assured us. "And Miss Rocco has her accounts and holdings hidden already."

I looked at her, and she smiled. "Let's go, shall we?"

Katie drove us to an apartment not far away. It was a quiet area, and as we went inside, the place had a generic, hotel-room sort of feel to it.

"I rented it pre-furnished," Katie told us. "I keep it in case I need to disappear, you know, if the paparazzi get too pushy or something like that."

"Yeah, sure." I told her I hadn't been in the limelight for decades, though I knew that it would have been nice to have someplace to disappear to when I had my meltdown.

"Two bedrooms, two baths, and a stocked fridge. I pay someone to keep it stocked," Katie went on, gesturing around. "I haven't been here in months, but there's a cleaning crew."

Arnold turned to her. "Thank you, Miss Rocco, you have helped us more than we could expect."

"Thanks, Arnold, you're a sweetheart." She smiled at him. I couldn't help a flare of jealousy.

He went to the kitchen and got out milk, eggs, and a blender. He hadn't had a protein drink in at least eight hours, so I suppose it was about that time.

I realized that left Katie and I standing in the living room alone.

"So, uh…" I trailed off, not certain what to say.

She arched an eyebrow at me. The fire had brought her age back somewhere around sixteen. Just about where she'd been when we had been on set together.

My mouth had gone dry. "You really mean what you said earlier—"

Wreckt started the blender. The loud noise startled me, and it pretty much made talking impossible.

"Come on." Katie pulled me into the bedroom and closed the door, the sound dropping off, so we could actually hear one another. "Sorry, what was that?"

Now I was alone with her in a bedroom. My brain froze up as I tried to think of the last time I had been alone with any woman, much less one who I liked this much.

"Do you really mean that you like… me?" I asked, waving down at myself.

She laughed. "I mean, you've got a certain nineties bad-boy look going that I liked at the time. I even had a little bit of a crush on you on set…"

"No way. I had a crush on you." I shook my head.

"Maybe I'm just a sucker for guys who need a lot of work." Katie laughed.

"I don't need a lot of work, I'm never going to get better," I protested. "This is *me*. I'm trapped in a sixteen-year-old body, complete with the hormones and the impulse control issues. I'm even stuck with the same crappy nineties haircut."

"I was wondering about that." She reached out and touched my hair. "It just grows back like that?"

I nodded. "It's like my body is fixed. Hair grows back to where it was and stops. My fingernails take a lot longer, but them, too. I've had teeth regrow, the whole works. I'm stuck. Most normal people, well, this all scares the hell out of them."

She arched an eyebrow. "You think *I'm* normal?"

"I mean normal-ish. You know, not a freak," I told her. "As you might realize, there were a few actors and others at various points in time who got really interested in me after... after what happened." I shuddered. "They liked the thought of dating an always-young teenage boy."

Katie made a face. "You want to be sure I'm not like that?"

I couldn't help but look away.

She caught my chin and gently turned my face toward her. "Eddie, I've been through that, in more ways than one. Right now, I'm sixteen. My body has reverted back to this age, and I'll stay this way as long as I can hold it. I ran into those same types, making movies. I even married one, God help me. Thankfully, I was able to walk away from that jackass, even though he was really hot, and we had some crazy chemistry."

She shook her head. "I like you for you, Eddie. More than most, I understand that the outside is just the dross. You might be in the body of a sixteen-year-old, but you are what, forty-five?"

"Yeah." I nodded.

"I don't *want* you for your body, Eddie. My body, here in a moderate period of time, will be that of an eighty-year-old woman. Will you still like me, then?"

"Of course I'll still like you," I protested.

"So, what's there to worry about? We're both consenting adults. We're both interested in one another. Anything else to add?"

"The fire thing terrifies me," I admitted. "When you lit off the flamethrower, I think I peed myself a bit."

She wrinkled her nose. "Yeah, you smell like sweat, blood, and a little bit of pee." She laughed and pointed at the bathroom. "The shower is there, how about we both get cleaned up?"

"You want to shower together?" I asked nervously.

She smiled. "Why, thank you for asking, Eddie, I will scrub your back if you'll scrub mine?"

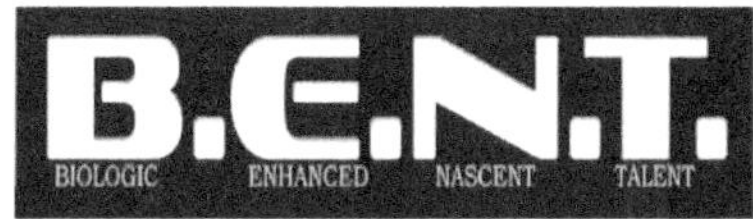

We lay in bed, afterward. I was exhausted, yet unable to sleep. My mind raced through everything going on and everything at stake.

There were actual stakes, now, too. Not just my miserable life, anyway, or Arnold Wreckt, who would be just as happy working at a gym and helping people get fit.

Katie was in this, now, too. So was Norm Linus and Clarence and…

"Does it hurt?" I asked.

Katie's head rested on my chest, and she answered sleepily, "Hmmm, no, it felt *really* good, especially when you…"

"No, I mean when you… when the fire consumes you," I told her.

She went still against me, and I could tell that my question had stirred her to fully awake. "No," she answered in a thoughtful tone. "It's like a glow, something I always feel, but when the fire hits me, it builds from the inside out and back. It's being reborn, rebuilt, and rejuvenated all at once."

"That sounds wonderful," I said, without any bitterness, though I felt a fair bit of envy.

"Does your regeneration hurt?" Katie asked softly.

"Indescribably," I told her. "I feel the injury, and then I feel my body pushing, prodding, and pulling everything back into place."

"I'm sorry." She hugged me as she said it.

"It's life," I told her, holding her close to me and feeling her breath on my chest. I didn't hurt at all, right now. I snorted, then said, "Really, I suppose Wreckt isn't the only Talent. You have your… phoenix thing. I regenerate a different way. Really, I guess you could say that my Talent is getting hurt."

She squeezed me in a hug as my laughter turned to a sob. I let tears roll down my cheeks, then, tears for the life I had lived, for the loneliness I had felt. For the pain, the trauma of a shitty childhood, and the consequences I had dealt with ever since.

It felt good to cry. I felt no shame in it, next to her. As she held on to me, I let the tears flow, and I felt safe, for the first time, possibly in my entire life.

We fell asleep that way.

Chapter 11

Katie had ordered us new clothes, and those showed up as Arnold and I were getting ready in the morning. She already had on a new black jumpsuit.

I had to ask, "Do you have a bunch of those? How is the one you had not all burned up?"

She winked at me. "You just want to see me with my clothes burned off."

I choked on my coffee and flushed, glancing at Arnold to see if he had noticed. He was making eggs and bacon, enough to feed a small army. He didn't look up at the byplay. I didn't think he had even noticed that we had gone to the bedroom together.

"They're a Nomex/Kevlar blend." She turned in a pirouette. "I like to wear them anyway. It's a little heavy, especially during the summer, but it is nice not to have to worry about my clothing going up if I do."

"Huh, that should provide protection, too. Isn't Kevlar bulletproof?" I asked.

"Bullet resistant and also flame resistant," Katie corrected me. "I don't know how *resistant* these are, but I'd rather not try getting shot if I can avoid it."

I nodded. "Yeah…"

I looked over at Arnold. "Breakfast ready, big guy?"

He came over and thumped two plates in front of us. I think he made me a full dozen eggs, and I had a stack of bacon. I started to tell him I wasn't that hungry, but then my stomach rumbled. I dug in. Across from me, Katie did as well. I shouldn't have been surprised at how both of us ate. I knew from various bumps and scrapes I had before all this that my healing burned up calories. I suppose it was the same for her, too.

I ate everything Arnold had cooked and drank three glasses of milk, besides. Arnold, meanwhile, had eaten everything on his plate and then gone back to the kitchen to make himself another shake.

I went to check out our new duds. I pulled out the first. It was a suit sized for Arnold. I squinted at her. "How did you get his measurements?"

"I have a good eye for such things. He'll need that if he needs to meet anyone in a professional way. There's one in there for you for the meeting with the finance people."

I pulled that one out. It was a bluish-gray. I started getting dressed in it and then looked at her incredulously. "This fits *really* well."

"You don't think all of what we were doing last night was just for fun? I got your measurements." She winked at me again. "*All* your measurements."

I coughed in embarrassment as I finished putting it on. There were shoes to match and even a tie. It was a nice silk one with little cartoon ghosts on it, and as I peered at it, I recognized them from the set of the movie we had been on together. It made me tear up. "This is the sweetest thing anyone has ever given me."

Katie laughed. "Well, you can return the favor by not turning into a jerk like all my other boyfriends or my ex-husband, deal?"

I could only nod in return. I wanted to admit to her that I probably was a jerk, but I couldn't make the words come out. I didn't think I could stand it if she walked away.

Arnold finished his shake and took his suit, heading into his room to change. He came out looking sharp, though his suit didn't fit him as well as mine, which gave me some gratification. I didn't want to think about Katie "measuring" him the way she had with me.

"I have been thinking about Bori." Arnold took a seat, the wooden chair groaning under his weight.

"Who?" Katie looked between us, clearly not understanding.

"Borislava." I rolled my eyes. "The Talent that the Russians are using as a bruiser. The woman who knocked Arnold through a wall… twice."

"They call her Bolshoy Borislava." Wreckt's eyes teared up a bit. "I looked it up, it means 'Great Borislava,' and Borislava means 'glorious warrior.' She is strong and strong-willed."

"Um… she's trying to kill us, bud," I reminded him.

"There is nothing personal to it," Wreckt told me. "She is doing what they make her do."

"You mooning over her could get us killed." I pointed at him. "You didn't even fight back when she came after us."

"I think it's sweet." Katie smiled.

I looked at her incredulously. "Sweet? She smashed me across the room back there. Any harder, and you would have had to scrape me up with a spatula."

"I watched the footage." Wreckt held up his hands. "I am sure that she pulled the punch."

I stared at him. "You think…" I had to sit down, or I might have hysterics. I frowned then. "You watched the footage?"

"It is all over the news," Arnold told me. "Here, look."

He turned on the TV. "I set it to record while you were both in bed."

I flushed scarlet as I realized that perhaps he had noticed where Katie and I had gone after all.

"Here's one I haven't watched yet." Arnold pulled up one of several shows.

"Tonight on *Datapoint*…" a serious-faced news anchor spoke. "Who are Eddie Connors and Arnold Wreckt? The overnight internet sensations appear to be the good guys. *Datapoint* has dug deeper, delving into the backgrounds of both Eddie Connors and Arnold Wreckt. What we have learned may surprise you…"

I frowned. "I don't like the sound of that…"

"When you dig into Eddie Connor's background, you find years of drug abuse, malicious accusations against big names in Hollywood, and even charges for arson, attempted murder, and insurance fraud," the news anchor went on.

I stood up from the couch. "You sonava…"

Arnold pushed me back down. "Quiet."

"With us today is criminal psychologist and former FBI profiler, Doctor Smith." The news anchor put extra emphasis on the man's title, as if that made him special or something. I'd dealt with plenty of "Doctors" in Hollywood who would do and say anything for enough money. "Doctor Smith, what is your profile for Connors?"

Smith was an older guy with gray hair, thick-rimmed glasses, and a serious expression. "What you need to understand is that as we peel back the layers, we see an increasingly dangerous personality manifest. As we see in the footage, Mister Connors has surgically maintained his appearance to that of when he was a child star. The alarming focus required to maintain such a feat speaks of a level of narcissism, and an unhealthy desire for attention."

"I'm BENT, you frigging moron," I growled.

"What you don't understand is that the rest of it paints him as a criminal mastermind. He has clearly manipulated events, going as far as to have his attackers walk into a clear ambush last night. I can only speculate on the identities, but they were clearly federal agents there to arrest Mister Connors for his crimes." Smith said it in a tone of condescension. "I hope you all will join me in a moment of silence for the families of those men who lost their lives."

"Half of them were Russian mobsters trying to kill us, the other half were black ops thugs who shot first!" I protested.

"Shush," Katie told me.

"It looks as if Mister Connors has further webbed Mister Wreckt into his schemes. Mister Wreckt is clearly below average in intelligence, a common feature with those of his Talent type," Doctor Smith went on.

"I will show him below average." Arnold clenched a fist.

"Connors is using Wreckt as his muscle in whatever criminal enterprise he's running," Doctor Smith went on. "The pair of them really need to be stopped."

"Interesting," the news anchor nodded, as if everything Doctor Smith had said were profound and accurate. He turned to the camera. "Is Eddie Connors a menace and threat? Is Wreckt a muscle-bound thug? Join us, as we take a deep-dive into their pasts, with a visit to people who know them personally. Starting with a woman who dated Connors over thirty years ago…"

"Okay, we've seen enough." I reached for the remote.

Katie snatched it out of Wreckt's hand and shot me a glare. "Try it."

I wisely kept my hands to myself.

"This is actress Alice Medio," the news anchor went on. "Alice, what can you tell our viewers about Eddie Connors?"

Alice looked at the camera. "I dated Eddie for almost two years."

"That was a relationship arranged by our agents because they thought it would drive interest in our careers," I gritted through my teeth.

"Shut it." Katie elbowed me in the ribs.

"During that time, I noticed he took a lot of medication…"

"*She* gave me half of the illegal ones," I muttered. "She was on more drugs than all the Rolling Stones *combined*."

"He also seemed unable to care about others. Like, once, I was trying to get him to back a project to house the homeless, and he blew me off," Alice went on.

I scowled at the television. "I was in the hospital, you crazy—"

Katie elbowed me again. I shut up.

"He barely ever listened to me when I talked about the importance of helping oppressed indigenous people in South Africa, and he wouldn't even get on the jet with me when I flew down to join a hunger strike to oppose the Apartheid."

"Thank you, Alice, do you have anything else to add?" the news anchor asked.

"I just want to encourage our viewers to cut back on their carbon emissions. I just flew back from a climate workshop in Milan, where we talked about pledges to save Earth. If just fifty people will give up their gas powered cars and pledge to walk or bike to work, we can remove as much as five hundred tons of carbon from the atmosphere."

"Thank you, Alice." The news anchor looked back at the screen. "Our research suggests that Eddie Connors is a dangerous, possibly violent man, with narcissistic tendencies and a grave lack of concern with others. Only time will tell how dangerous he is."

Katie turned off the TV and looked at me, her expression serious. "Should I be concerned?"

My eyes went wide, and I felt panic rise up inside. "You can't tell me that you believe any of that—"

She burst out laughing. "Oh, please, your *expression*, Eddie." She waved at the television. "They pulled out Alice Medio? She's seriously crazy. I *cannot* believe you dated her."

I looked down at the floor. "My parents and my agent set it up. They wanted to try and stir up some more public interest. Then *Roboslayer Three* fell through, and they hoped that having that relationship might mitigate some of the damage to my public appearance."

"I bet she was a bundle of fun." Katie shook her head.

"I mean, she was nice." I shrugged. "Not all there, though, not terribly bright, and quick to talk any line that people put in her head. I haven't talked to her in decades. To be honest, her flying off to South Africa or whatever was the last time I saw her. She called me, after"—I flinched—"after what happened, when I was in the hospital. That was when she tried to get me on that project. I tried asking her for help, explaining what I was going through."

I shook my head. "She thought I didn't care about her project, her cause, and she hung up on me. It was sort of the final lesson in my life about people not giving a crap."

Katie reached out and squeezed my hand. "I care."

"I know," I told her. We kissed.

"Ahem." Arnold cleared his throat.

I realized that our kiss had been going on perhaps a bit longer and a bit further than I would have if I had remembered he was right there.

"Sorry." I turned beet red, and my face burned.

Katie didn't look sorry at all.

"So, we can see what the mainstream media is saying, let's see what the internet has," Katie told us, bringing up BlueTube on the television.

"Why would they say anything different?" I asked. From painful experience with the media as a teenager, I figured everyone would just repeat whatever salacious gossip the media shared.

"No one takes the big news companies at face value anymore." Katie laughed. "Well, no one with half a brain, anyway. Here we go… Chuck Ratan, of the Chuck Ratan Experience. He's got a piece on you already."

"Who?" I asked.

She pulled up the video, Chuck was a bald guy with a relaxed expression. She hit play.

"So, guys, like these two come out of nowhere, right?" Chuck laughed. "I mean, no one heard of

Eddie Connors since I was in high school. He was that dweeby kid with the hair and the smart mouth."

I wanted to punch Chuck right in the face.

"And Wreckt, who's talked about Wreckt since then, either? Right? And now the governor of Illinois says they're white supremacists and tried to assassinate them? And there's FBI profilers hopping on *Datapoint* saying they're criminal masterminds? I don't buy it. Look, if Connors was a criminal mastermind, why wait thirty years to launch your criminal career? Why try to knock off a pair of corrupt politicians to do it?"

Okay, maybe he's not so bad.

"I've watched their feed, man." Chuck laughed. "They don't look like criminal masterminds. Connors looks like he's doing his best to stay alive. Lots of action, I'll give them that, and the guy managing their tech, I want to hire him, no offense to my crew, but this guy manages cameras and the feed, all live, really nice, man. Criminal masterminds? Dude wouldn't be getting gut shot with a shotgun in front of two hundred thousand viewers if he was a criminal mastermind."

"Holy crap, he's not telling the official story." I stared at the television in surprise. Last time I had been in the news, everyone had run the official story, almost word for word. Not one person had questioned it. To everyone, from the paparazzi to the local news outlets to the major newspapers, I was a drug-addled loser who had let fame and fortune get to his head, stolen a car, made some wild allegations, and then got arrested.

"See?" Katie paused the show. "If he's running this, and you're putting your stream out live, then big media can't bury this, no matter who is pushing it."

"Okay, so what do we do, then?" I was still struggling with the idea that people might actually believe us. I mean, it wasn't flattering that this Chuck guy thought I was an incompetent idiot, but that was still better than the official line that I was some kind of criminal psycho.

Arnold smiled. "We make the movie."

Katie gave me a nod. "We make the movie. You need to meet the finance guys."

I took a deep breath. "Okay, let's go meet the finance guys."

"What's the worst that can happen?" Arnold laughed.

I turned and glowered at him. "Stop saying that! Don't you know it is bad luck? Next thing I know, someone's going to say 'good luck.'"

I slapped my hands over my mouth as I realized what I had said. No one said that in relation to show business. I had just cursed us.

I heard a helicopter sweep past low overhead.

Chapter 12

The helicopter was only the start of it. In the hallway outside the door, I heard boot steps and shouts.

I turned to Katie. "Does this place have a back door?"

She shook her head. "I never thought I'd need one."

"I am the back door." Arnold rose up, walked back, and kicked the back wall of the apartment out.

"Sorry about your apartment's damage deposit," I told Katie.

"Don't mess up your suit." She punched me in the shoulder. "Also, no getting shot until after the meeting! Oh, and turn on your camera!"

"Yes, Mother." I laughed at her, feeling semi-hysterical as we ran for it. I grabbed my phone as we ran through the kitchen.

I heard them blow in the front door of the apartment as we jumped down into the parking lot. An armed man turned toward us. He had "police" on his armor. "Arnold, gentle!" I warned him.

He "gently" threw the man into the wall, hard enough to leave him stunned but hopefully not hard enough to have killed him.

A police helicopter buzzed by overhead. Another one circled the other way. That one was all black with no tail markings, I noticed.

About the same time I noticed that, the side door opened, and someone opened up with a machine gun.

Katie and I ran for it as bullets tore through the cars in the parking lot. She got to her SUV.

"Leave it, that thing will shred us!" I protested.

"I told you it's got *all* the upgrades, get in!" Katie shouted.

I didn't argue. I hoped she knew what she was doing as I climbed in. Wreckt jumped in the back seat behind us.

Bullets smashed into the side of the vehicle, sounding like steel rain or really big hail.

The outer layers of glass splintered a bit, but they held. "Fully armored," she told us. "Like I said, a Saudi prince has the same model."

She put it into gear, and we drove forward toward the parking lot entrance. Some police tried to block the way, but they dodged out of her way as she revved the engine and drove straight at them.

"Oh, crap"—I pointed ahead of us on the street—"is that a tank?"

"Get the camera on it," Katie answered as she drove right at it. It didn't have treads, but it had like six wheels and a weird-shaped hull. It turned sideways as we raced at it, and I saw it fire smoke or gas canisters at us.

Katie drove straight at it like she was going to ram, and I found myself bracing myself for impact. At the last minute, as we drove into the smoke, she swerved to the side, up over the curb, across the sidewalk, and around the corner.

"I was hoping I could get out and punch it," Wreckt complained from the back seat.

"They're just cops. We don't want to kill any of them," I reminded him.

Katie drove the big SUV like a race car, and I couldn't help but clutch at the seat as she took a corner faster than I thought possible.

"How does this thing go so fast?" I stuttered.

"It's got a twin turbocharged V8. We can go *much* faster." Katie grinned.

The two helicopters were behind us. The one continued to fire its machine gun at us as we raced down the street.

"These idiots are going to shoot innocent people," Wreckt growled. I turned the camera on him as he went on, "Those are innocent people, be careful!"

I panned the camera up to the sunroof, just in time for a spray of bullets to rake across the top of the SUV.

"I'll try to lose them. Maybe they'll stop shooting if they don't have a shot," Katie told us. She accelerated faster, blowing through a set of traffic lights. Our earbuds were still in the car, and I fumbled grabbing them out of the center console and passing them around. "Hello, hello, this thing on?" I asked.

"I've got you guys," Lawrence yawned in my ear. "Can't a guy get a little rest?"

"They're shooting at us," I said unnecessarily.

"I'm aware." Lawrence sounded unimpressed. "Try and aim the camera up at the helicopters. I would love some more footage of that."

I mumbled something under my breath as I tried to angle up through the sunroof again.

"Do we have anything I can throw?" Wreckt asked.

"You can't hit a helicopter!" I protested.

"You are right." He nodded. "It might crash into someone when it falls."

"No, I meant I've seen your throwing arm. Your aim sucks; you grew up playing soccer."

"Sick burn, brah." Katie laughed. "Tell it like it is."

"Seriously, he couldn't play basketball to save his life," I told her.

Wreckt glowered at me. He didn't argue, though. One of the only movies I had landed for us had been a sports movie, and he had been so bad at throwing and catching a ball they had needed a stunt double for that part.

Katie went over a curb and bounced me hard, just as bullets thumped into the side from the helicopter. "How many hits will this thing take?" I couldn't help but look at the starred glass.

"It is rated for up to three hundred impacts," Katie said in a matter-of-fact voice.

"How are you so calm?" I asked, my voice squeaking a bit. I put the camera on her as I looked at her.

"I'm terrified," Katie admitted. "I would love to have a screaming panic fit. They're shooting at us with a machine gun from a *helicopter* in downtown Chicago. Somehow, *we* are supposed to be the bad guys?"

More bullets impacted the rear. "I think they are aiming for the tires," Arnold told us.

"That's unfortunately smart of them." Katie nodded. "Hold on, I'm going to try to lose them in the underpasses up here."

She floored it, and we wove through traffic in a blur. I brought the camera around as we flashed past two police cars, their lights and sirens on, and Katie managed to miss both of them by mere inches. She took a corner, went under a bridge, and swung hard to make another turn. Then she pulled into an alleyway. "Cut the feed," she told me.

I shut off the camera.

Katie looked over at me. "I'm going to drop you here. It's a half block to Linus's office. There's an underground parking garage down this way that we'll hide in. Call us when the meeting is done."

I leaned over and kissed her. She pushed me back. "More of that later. Go or you'll be late."

I got out, and she drove away. I straightened my suit and walked out of the alley, keeping my head down and walking as calmly as I could manage.

A couple of cop cars went past, their lights and sirens going. I could hear the helicopter sweep by overhead. I kept my head down.

"Are they okay?" I asked, not sure if Lawrence could hear me.

Apparently, having the phone on me was good enough.

"They're fine," Lawrence yawned. "Do well at the meeting, okay? I'm going to try and get a nap in."

I muttered something under my breath as he went silent.

I made it to the building with Norm Linus's office without any issues. I felt like the security guard in the lobby kept looking at me as I waited for the elevator, but he went back to the game on his phone as the doors opened.

Linus's office was about midway up, and I checked the time on my phone as I stepped off the elevator, realizing that I'd managed to be just a few minutes late. *Great way to set a good impression…*

I hurried to Linus's office and opened the door, "Uh, sorry I'm late."

"Eddie, not a problem, not a problem at all," Linus told me as I came in. "Clarence was just finishing up on the details of his script."

There were three guys seated on Linus's cheap office couch. All three wore suits that probably cost more than the office's rent for the entire year. One of them looked Middle Eastern, one looked Asian, and the third had a cowboy hat on.

"…and that's when the queen, she like realizes she really needs the dude, so she sets him up as a duke so they can get married." Clarence was going on.

"I am confused," the Asian one said. "Why is she breaking the societal and cultural normative?"

"It's 'cause she loves him, dawg," Clarence told him. "It talks to the artificial nature of societal boundaries and the dichotomy of male-female relationships versus societal power. Also, she really likes his big—"

"Yeah, yeah, she wants to ride his bronco." The cowboy waved a hand. He looked over at me. "You're the one with the action script?"

"Yes." I nodded.

All three of them stared at me.

Linus elbowed me.

I started talking, "Yeah, so there's this strongman, played by Arnold Wreckt. He's down on his luck, hasn't done very well. Him and his, uh, personal trainer, are trying to make a go of things, and they run afoul of the Russian mob and some crooked politicians."

"Why both at once?" the Middle Eastern guy asked.

"The bad guys were in a meeting, exchanging money for the politicians looking the other way while the mob arranges to buy real estate cleared out by riots or something," I told them. "The Russians brought in the strongman because he beat up one of their mob enforcers."

"Huh, it seems dumb of the Russian to bring these two to his meeting, as potential witnesses"—the Middle Easterner shrugged—"but everyone hates the Russians right now, so that plays to societal prejudices. At least you're not making it the military veteran or the Arab as the bad guy." He laughed at that.

"Is there a love interest?" the Asian guy asked.

"Oh, yeah." I nodded. "Two of them, the, uh, trainer with this bombshell, she's going to be played by Katie Rocco…"

"I loved her in that creepy family movie, the one with the catchy tune." The cowboy nodded. "She hasn't been in a lot, lately. Are you sure you can get her?"

"Yeah, pretty sure." I nodded. "The other one is between Wreckt and one of the mob enforcers. She's a Talent, and he likes her strength. They're on opposite sides, so we're still trying to make it work."

"Hmmm, some kind of redemption arc." The Asian nodded. "That could be good."

"What about action?" The cowboy asked. "We need explosions, gunfire, the whole deal. None of the CGI crap that Hollywood does, real stunts, with real actors."

Linus slapped me on the shoulder. "Eddie here has made sure there's these off-book Feds, real black operations guys, flying around in helicopters firing off machine guns and blowing up buildings."

"Interesting…" The Asian frowned. "How do they tie in?"

"A case of mistaken identity," I told him. "I'm not entirely sure"—Linus elbowed me in the side, and I coughed—"that is, I am pretty sure I know how to tie that part up in the end."

"Fantastic." The Middle Eastern guy nodded. "The strongman's love interest, is she a big woman?"

"Uh… we're trying to sign the actress, but probably." I looked at Linus, who gave me a nod.

"Good, Hollywood too often casts these petite women. They do not look as if they could lift a fork, much less throw men around. We need more actresses like that Carano woman, fierce and strong and with curves in all the right areas."

The cowboy laughed and slapped the arm of the couch. "He's right, there. Yeah, I'm in on this. Especially since you have some actors lined up. They're good with *both* scripts?"

Linus nodded. "Oh, yeah, it's a package deal. The actors love both scripts. I'm already talking with the agent representing them."

Seeing as how I was their agent, I nodded in agreement.

The three of them stood. "Alright, Linus, you've got us sold." The cowboy gave him a nod. "Been a pleasure, gents. Have your people call mine to set up the details. Oh, and you'll do some product placement stuff for our companies, right?"

"Not a problem at all. We'll make sure that's worked in." Linus nodded.

They walked out, the Asian and the Middle Eastern guys discussing where to get lunch.

"That went well." I looked at Linus.

He slumped down in his desk chair like a wet noodle. "You showed up just in time. C-dawg here had buried them in details. Clarence, you got to play to their interests, man. You almost killed us, there."

Clarence looked sheepish. "Sorry, dawg, I got nervous, and the more I talked, the less they looked like they cared."

"It's fine." Linus waved a hand. "Now, we're good. The three of them could fund both movies from their slush funds. They all got screwed over by various executives in Hollywood on the past few movies they backed, too, so they're willing to stick it in their eyes and fund this."

"How'd they get screwed over?" I frowned.

"They're approaching movies as an investment. If the movie makes money, they make money," Linus told me.

"Right…" I frowned.

"Well, dirty secret here, but most movies in Hollywood are made to fail; they *never* make money. They're a huge tax deduction. The bookkeeping for this stuff is murkier than you can imagine. Did they spend a hundred million or three hundred million on advertisements? Ten million or forty million on sets and costumes? Hard to say. It all gets destroyed afterward, anyway, oops, there's no evidence other than the paper and invoices."

I frowned. "Wait, so you're saying they intentionally lose money?"

"Yeah, other than a big hit here and there to look right. Even then, for the investors, it's a net *loss*. It's a tax write-off. Those three like movies, that's why they came. Most of the big money investors don't give a crap, they want the movie to take a loss so the costs are on paper. Meanwhile, their companies get product placement for free advertising, the investors' immediate family members get cushy, well-paying jobs, and actors with the politics they like get fat paychecks."

"That's even scummier than I remember." I scowled.

"It's the game." Linus shrugged. "The big money over time is in the residuals and overseas. There's two billion people in Asia, another billion in Europe. They get the gradual income from that, and it adds up. These three actors bad-mouthed their companies on the red-carpet, and the producers they went with didn't balance things right. The last few movies made money, which left these guys burned at tax-time."

"So, they want to go with us?" I asked. "They're expecting our movies to flop?"

"Not at all," Linus assured me. "They expect them to lose money. There's a world of difference, there. We'll have to pay actors, sets, props, costumes. We'll need to do all the action live, with stuntmen, real explosions, helicopters. This all gets extremely expensive. They want us to take their money and spend *all* of it. To move it around and spend more than we think we can earn. Let me worry about the books. You're an agent, anyway. I don't want you too in-depth on the money side of things.

"The basis of it, as long as the movie *loses* money, everyone is happy. The investors get their tax write-off, everyone else gets paid, and over time, we can still get residuals. We're going to spend *a lot* of money, Eddie. We're going to cast Arnold Wreckt with a huge signing bonus, same for Katie, and they're going to invest most of that in the movie, too."

"Wait, what?" I frowned.

"Probably in different movies, the pay from one going to the other." Linus pointed at me and then at Clarence. "That looks a little more legitimate."

"But… if they're going to lose money, why?" I stared at him in incomprehension. The idea of deliberately losing money gave me a headache. For the past thirty years, I hadn't ever had enough money to do more than scrape by.

"Because otherwise, the fascists in the IRS are going to take every penny they can," Linus told me. "We'll juggle the money around with multiple investment companies and production companies, and at the end of it, Wreckt Productions is going to be losing money on paper, and you and Wreckt—and of course, Lawrence, Katie, Clarence, and everyone else—will be living comfortable."

"I don't understand," I protested.

"No one does. It is money, politics, and taxes. Believe me, those bureaucratic fucks at the IRS want it as obtuse and confusing as possible. It makes it so their rich friends can hide their money while the little guy gets squeezed. Like Hollywood, it is a game, and the game is rigged." Linus looked out the window. "Alright, so, we have money lined up. I didn't watch all your live footage from last night. Did you get anywhere on getting the heat off you both?"

"Not really," I told him. "Lawrence didn't fill you in?"

"I was prepping for this meeting." Linus shook his head. "I didn't want any distractions."

"The black ops guys tried to murder me. I guess they think I'm some shape-changing most wanted guy," I told him.

Linus sat up, his eyes going wide behind his thick glasses. "They think *you* are Alexander Lloyd?"

"Yeah, I think that's his name." I scratched my head. "Pretty nuts, huh?"

"Holy shit, that's…" Linus stared at me for a moment, then pulled off his glasses and cleaned them on his safari vest and put them back on. "Just to be clear, and I'm asking this from a purely professional curiosity… you really aren't him, right? You wouldn't lie to me about that, right?"

I blinked at him. "Uh, no, Norm, I'm not this Lloyd guy."

He stared at me, as if he weren't entirely certain I was telling the truth.

"If I was a shapechanger, I'm pretty sure I would have bounced out of this town as soon as stuff got hot." I laughed. "I sure as hell wouldn't stick around and try to make a movie. How stupid would this guy have to be to stick around if the secret organization after him knew exactly where he was?"

Linus still didn't look entirely convinced.

"Yo, dawg, that shapechanger dude is a bad man. I heard he murdered a whole human trafficking group in New York just a few weeks ago," Clarence spoke up from where he was looking over his script. "I mean, Eddie isn't exactly a fighter."

Linus looked at him and then back at me. "True enough. Too bad. I mean, I like you, Eddie, but if Lloyd had taken your place, wow, the opportunity to interview him… He's a legend, took on the FBI, the CIA, the NSA… he's a ghost."

"Huh, sounds like we need his help." I rubbed at my face, wishing I could grow even a goatee. "I've got no idea what to do about the black ops guys. Even if we clear our names from the governor and the mayor, the Feds can just issue warrants for us, and we're toast."

"Maybe not." Linus tapped his nose and pointed at me. "We're putting all this footage out there. It shows them coming after you all without any regards for collateral damage or rule of law. They have to try and spin that or worry about exposing themselves. If they issue warrants for your arrest, they're going public. Also, whatever case of mistaken identity they have now, that's only going to last so long. Especially if you, as their target, drop off the radar, or the *real* Lloyd pops up elsewhere."

"That would be handy," I mused. "Say, do you think he might do that just to mess with them?"

"I dunno, man." Clarence shook his head. "He's, like, a stone-cold killer. More likely he'd come after you for pretending to be him and then…" He jerked his thumb across his throat and made a *hurk* noise.

I didn't like the sound of that. I mean, what kind of psycho-killer was this guy that *everyone* wanted him dead? *Shit, maybe I need to think about hiding from him, too…*

"I think the biggest thing, right now, is for you to focus on the main threat, the corrupt Chi-town politicians and the former Soviet-bloc communist assholes pulling their strings," Linus told me. "Find a way to pull them all together in one spot, we air all their dirty laundry, and bam, there we go."

Clarence nodded. "That's how I would write it."

I snorted. "Alright, then, let's go make a movie."

Chapter 13

I met up with Wreckt and Katie an hour or so later. She had parked them in the lowest level of the underground parking garage. I was surprised she even had a cell phone signal down here, but she had sent a text to me with where to find them, and I was able to follow her directions with no issues.

I had just come down a stairwell and was behind them, out of their line of sight behind the vehicle. I should have called out to them, but I was curious what they were talking about.

"…think you're into her a little too fast, is all I am saying, Arnold." Katie was talking to Arnold over the hood of the SUV as I walked up. "I don't want you to get hurt."

"I can't help it," Wreckt told her. "She is strong, capable, and she clearly knows what she wants."

"You've talked with her for all of thirty seconds, most of that while she was trying to kill you," Katie told him. "A few encounters are hardly enough to base a relationship upon."

"Like you and Eddie?" Wreckt joked.

I was still in the stairwell, and I froze, scared to death of what she was going to say in response to that.

"Arnold, Eddie and I might not have spent much time together, but we *grew up* together, in a lot of ways. We knew the same people, we had the same shitty experiences, and we were shaped by similar things. I can look at Eddie and see a mirror of what I went through, and he sees the same thing. We're different people, but we understand one another at a level that's hard to describe."

My heart swelled up in my chest, and I felt tears fill my eyes. Katie had every opportunity there to agree, to discount our nascent relationship. She had done the opposite, and I only hoped that if I were in her shoes, I would have said it as well. *Probably not, I always suck at saying what I really feel. I'd probably make some lame smart-ass comment, and she would hear me and never want to see me again.*

"Then you know exactly how I feel when I look at Borislava," Wreckt told her.

I felt a shock at that. People often underestimated Arnold Wreckt's intelligence. Hell, often enough, *I* did so. It was easy to forget that behind that muscle and focus on his physique, there was a mind that ran like a machine, albeit, a very focused machine. The dude read books on fitness while lifting weights and doing cardio, for God's sake.

Arnold spoke, his harsh voice implacable, "She has been molded and shaped by her environment, forced to become strong and physically powerful. She has had to fight for herself and her family. She has had to train herself, with little help, and I can see all of that when I look at her. She also does not like the people she is working for, but she has no other choice."

That, I felt, was my cue.

I took a few steps back, going up the stairs and calling down, "Hey, guys, you sure you parked far enough down here?" I made a big deal of coming down the last steps.

I don't think either of them entirely bought it. I had been out of the acting business for a while, I suppose. That was fine, I just didn't want them to think I had been hanging out here in the shadows the entire time. That's the kind of thing a creeper would do.

"So, we're good on the investors. We've got the money to make the movies." I flashed them two thumbs up.

"Excellent." Arnold rubbed his hands together. "That is fantastic, Eddie. Good work."

"Even better," I told him, "remember how I gave Borislava a business card?"

"I think I missed that." Wreckt rubbed his chin.

"She had just knocked you through the back wall of the building, so…" I shrugged. "Anyway, she emailed me. She wants to meet."

"That is great!" Wreckt's smile went ear to ear.

"This is probably a trap." Katie rolled her eyes.

"Almost definitely." I nodded. "But it's also an opportunity. Either Arnold can overpower her, or we can convince her long enough not to fight us that we can talk."

"You think you can pitch her around to helping us?" Katie raised an eyebrow.

"Potentially." I nodded. "I mean, I'm great at making deals."

She and Wreckt both stared at me, as if they were waiting for a punchline.

I looked between them. "I mean, I'm your agent!"

Wreckt frowned. "Eddie, I hate to mention it, but there are numerous times you haven't been the best as my agent. You try 100 percent, and you're my friend, and that goes a long way, but…"

I looked over at Katie. "Come on, I mean, at least you're going to have me as…" I trailed off as I saw her guilty expression.

"Look, Eddie," Katie told me, "I *really* like you. That said, after everything I've been through, I have a strict no-sex-with-my-agent policy. I'm sure you can understand that."

My lips pressed into a flat line as I thought about the reasons *why* she might have that kind of policy. I gave her a nod, though, because I understood the importance of a policy like that.

"So, either we stop having sex, and you can be my agent, or we keep our relationship, and I use a different agent," Katie told me in a firm tone.

I frowned. "But…"

"Eddie, our relationship can be purely professional, or it can be something deeper and more rewarding. I chose the deeper one. Are you saying I should rethink that?"

In the face of losing her versus the little bit of success and money I'd get out of being her agent, I knew exactly which way I was going to go.

Plus, well, it had been a *long* time since I had sex with anyone.

"I guess I can live without being your agent," I answered.

She stepped forward, and we kissed. "Oh, good, because I thought we might be getting serious."

"What did Bori have to say?" Wreckt interrupted any further necking.

"She said she wants you and me to meet her." I cleared my throat and stepped back from Katie, though I still held her hands, and she held mine.

"She gave me an address and a time. If we leave soon, we can make it there. It's someplace out of the way, no big crowds of people in case things go bad." I looked over at him to see if he understood what that meant.

He nodded. "She would not want to endanger innocents if she could avoid it."

I didn't know about that. She had swatted a few of the FBI guys and several of those black ops guys. Then again, they hadn't seemed all that innocent, so who knew?

"Anyway, I figured you and I would go there. If it is an ambush, you fight through it, I film it and run and hide when necessary…" I was really hoping it wouldn't be a fight. Bolshoy Borislava hit *hard*. "If it's not an ambush, if she really wants to talk, then I…"

Wreckt cleared his throat and looked at me sternly.

"…that is, *we* talk to her," I finished. "If we can turn her, then we have an in as far as the Russians, at least."

"That's one part of the problem." Katie nodded. "You still don't have anything to clear either of you from the police and government, though."

"Yeah, I'm hoping all that will blow over. Linus brought up a good point: we've been streaming them attacking us, so maybe they'll realize that it's not working and drop it all," I told them.

Katie glanced at Arnold. "Do you want to tell him?"

"He would take it better from you," Wreckt told her.

"Tell me what?" I asked suspiciously.

"It came through a little while ago. Here, I'll pull it up on my car's screen, it's bigger than the phone, and it gets better reception." Katie went over, and we all climbed into her Mercedes. "And… here we are."

She brought up a video link from some local news station. The fat guy was making a statement, "I've now issued orders for a statewide manhunt for Eddie Connors and Arnold Wreckt. This morning, the two of them evaded numerous police and federal agents tasked with their capture. Their flagrant disregard for the safety of others shows that they are a menace to the good people of the State of Illinois."

"Governor, has there been any more about possible domestic terror ties with Connors?" a reporter asked.

"Yes, and we are continuing to investigate those ties. Next question," the governor went on.

"That was a terrible response. They were both very scripted." Arnold shook his head. "I could be a better governor than this guy."

"You weren't born in the States. I don't think you can be a governor." I frowned. *Or was that Presidents? I knew I should have got my GED at least.*

"Shut up and listen, you two," Katie snapped. We had missed a couple more of the scripted questions and answers.

"Governor, what kind of resources are you allocating to this?" another reporter asked.

This one wasn't on the script, I think, and the governor blinked and blurted, "All the resources. Our best people, state troopers, even the National Guard."

"Wait," a reporter asked, "you're calling up the National Guard for these two fugitives? What about the riots and looting that Chicago was subject to in the past couple of years?"

"Uh, those mostly peaceful protests didn't warrant this kind of response. Next question," the governor stuttered and pointed at one of the reporters up front from one of the major media companies.

At this point, the press had the scent of blood though, and another reporter shouted from the side, "Governor, why are you expending so many resources on these two when we have rampant crime problems here in Chicago?"

"Next question!" he barked.

"Governor, is there any truth to the accusations that Mister Karmazov has made illegal campaign donations to you and the mayor to support his purchase of large areas of real estate here in Chicago?"

"No further questions!" The governor stepped back from the podium and shoved his way off the stage as reporters descended like piranhas.

I was smiling. "That's great, right? They're questioning his story."

"You missed the part where he's calling up the National Guard," Katie reminded me.

I snorted. "National Guard, they're like, what, part-time Army? Like cooks and mechanics and that sort of thing, right? What's the big deal?"

Katie sighed and pulled up her phone, speaking into the search engine, "Query, how many National Guardsmen are in the Illinois National Guard?"

"There are over eleven thousand members of the Illinois National Guard," her phone answered.

"That's a lot of part-timers," Wreckt said in a somber tone.

"Query, what units are in the Illinois National Guard?" Katie glared at me as she said it.

"The Illinois National Guard includes the Thirty-Third Infantry Brigade Combat Team, with three combat battalions and an artillery regiment, the one-hundred-and-sixth combat aviation regiment, the one-hundred-and-twenty-third field artillery regiment…"

"Okay, okay, I got it, that sounds really freaking scary." I held up my hands. I wasn't even sure what "combat aviation" included, whether that was jet fighters or helicopters or what. I was pretty sure that field artillery was cannons, though I hadn't thought anyone used cannons and stuff like that anymore. I thought they fought wars with smart bombs and fighter jets.

I had no idea how many people were in a brigade or battalion or any of that. "At least they don't have tanks," I half-muttered.

"Query, does the Illinois National Guard have tanks?" Katie glared at me.

"Yes, the—"

"Okay!" I snapped. "What do you want me to do about it?"

Her phone answered, "I'm sorry, what was that? I didn't catch it."

Katie snorted and turned off her search software, and she arched an eyebrow at me.

"I wonder what would happen if I hit a tank?" Arnold clenched one fist in the back seat.

"Let's hope it doesn't come up," Katie said while still looking at me. "I want you to take this seriously. The media is after the governor, now. What happens with people like him when they get desperate?"

I immediately thought about Harvey Moore and how he had reacted after I accused him of trying to coerce me into sex. He'd gone after me, accused me of slander and defamation, tried to sue me for damages, and he had made it so I couldn't get a job in *any* movie…

"They go full-on attack mode." I rubbed at my eyes, feeling overwhelmed.

"Yeah, and this joker has who knows how many state troopers, the Chicago Police, and eleven thousand National Guardsmen at his beck and call," Katie told us.

"We don't want to fight them, either." Wreckt gave a sigh. "They aren't part of this, so we should avoid hurting them."

"Yeah." I rubbed my forehead, fighting a headache. All my good feelings from the meeting with the finance guys had evaporated. "Alright, what do we do?"

"We try to stay off the radar," Katie told us. "I've got someone bringing my other SUV. It's got tinted windows, and hopefully they won't be after it. You two will go to this meeting and try to find out how to nail this Russian guy after you both. Hopefully when he goes down, it will take the mayor and governor."

I nodded. "This sounds like a plan. What will you do?"

Katie smiled at me. "I'll be ready to come in and save you both when it all goes horribly wrong."

"What do you think?" Wreckt asked me a bit later as we drove toward the meeting with Borislava. He was driving, which was just as well; I wasn't a good driver at the best of times.

"I think that this has gotten a little out of hand." I was flipping through the phone, checking emails, checking how we were trending on social media, and occasionally reading what news bloggers and the media had to say about us.

"We just wanted to make a movie." I hated the whiny tone of my voice.

"Do you still want to run for it?" Wreckt looked over at me.

I thought about it. I thought about Katie and how I wouldn't be able to have any kind of life with her if I was on the run. I thought about the assholes in Hollywood who had made it so Wreckt and I were persona non grata. I thought about the corrupt politicians who would go on doing whatever they wanted if Wreckt and I skipped town.

"No, we need to fight this." I didn't know how I *could* fight it, but I felt like I had to do it. I couldn't run the rest of my life. In a lot of ways, I felt like that was what I had been doing, running from fights I couldn't win. It was time to stop running.

"Good, I couldn't leave without Bori, and this feels like the right thing to do." Wreckt smiled.

"She still probably wants to stomp both of us flat," I had to point out. My whole body hurt at the thought of her hitting me again.

"She doesn't, trust me," Wreckt assured me.

"Well… here's the moment of truth," I told him as we pulled up in front of an old power transfer building. I checked my phone, making sure of the battery charge and that the camera with all its streaming stuff was ready. We had coordinated with Lawrence so this was all going to a file somewhere, rather than going out live. That way he could air it later.

After all, if Borislava did want to switch sides, then we didn't want her boss to know that.

We got out, Arnold kicking a bit of rusted machinery. "It saddens me to see how decrepit this city has become. They used to make things here."

"Yeah, well"—I shrugged—"maybe they'll build it back, better." I didn't think much of the current governor, for obvious reasons. I somehow doubted that the system that had put him in charge would replace him with anyone better.

I wasn't going to change the system, though. I just wanted to clear my name. I didn't care about the political alignment of the people in charge or what they said they stood for. I just didn't want the ones taking money from the Russian mob to be in charge anymore.

We walked through the doors. The interior was wide and open. Heavy machinery had been pulled out, leaving a forlorn, empty look to the big structure.

"Hello?" I called out. "We're here, alone, as requested."

I tensed, half expecting gunfire or something similar as a response.

Instead, a single figure stepped forward out of the shadows on the far side of the space. It was Borislava, in her more petite merely-six-feet-tall form. "Thank you for meeting me," she greeted us in a heavily-accented voice. "I wasn't sure if you would come."

"Of course." Wreckt smiled at her. "Why wouldn't we?"

"You have been… kind to me." Borislava walked closer. "And your friend has offered me a job… Is this in jest or in truth?"

"We're making two movies," I went into pitch mode. "We can definitely write you in one or both of them." If I could talk her around, then we were money.

"And you…" She turned to face Wreckt. "You have been… kind to me. Why?"

"I feel as if I know you." Wreckt's voice went gentle. "You have had to fight for everything you have. You are strong, people judge you by that and that alone. They do not see you for the person inside, for the effort you have put into it, for what it costs you."

Her expression shifted. "That is sweet of you, but it only makes this harder. I have to bring both of you to Anton Karmazov."

"Why?" I asked. "You mentioned your family before. Does he have them or something?"

She nodded. "They are hostages to my good behavior. If I step out of line, he will kill them."

Wreckt's expression shifted. "Where does he have them? Maybe we can find them and set them free." There was such a look and tone of earnestness to him that I wanted to kick him in the shin, but I also didn't want to break my foot.

She shook her head. "That is kept secret. He moves them around and keeps them separate. Both my sisters, their Talents are useful to him, as is mine, in different ways. We get the chance to talk by phone, once a week, just for a few minutes. If one of us steps out of line, the others will be hurt."

"Are they like you?" Wreckt asked in a soft voice.

"No, they have different Talents. I have protected them." Borislava shook her head. "We come from Ukraine. From the… issues there. Karmazov's people, they offered to get us here to the United States to work, in exchange for money. They took our passports, took our documents. They found out we were Talents, and that was when everything changed, and they forced us to work for him."

"I will make him pay," Wreckt promised. His fists clenched, and it sounded like someone crushing gravel.

"You can't, you do not understand." Borislava stepped back from him, shaking her head. "He has promised me that my sisters and I will go free when I bring you. As soon as I tell him that I have you, he will bring them. It is the only way that they and I can be free."

"We can help you." I stepped past Arnold, patting him on the shoulder to let him know that I was on his side. "If they are present, then we can free them. This Karmazov jerk, you can't trust him, anyway. Everything I have seen about him suggests he just plans to keep them and you, regardless of any deals he offers."

She scowled at me. "Do you think I don't realize that? I'm not stupid. This is just the only route left open to me."

Wreckt held up his hands. "Look, Bori, let us help you. I know what it is like, to be viewed only as muscle, to never have a chance to be seen as more, to be used by people who want me only for the outside. We are not like that."

She shook her head. "Why should I trust *you*?"

"Because I care." Wreckt's voice went gentle. "I was just like you, until one day, I saw someone hurt Eddie, and I realized there were more important things than doing what I was told and hoping for table scraps. Men and women are not animals, we should not be kept and treated like prize stock. You are a woman, Bori, a beautiful woman, who deserves to be free. Not to be kept as a prize."

"You… you think I am beautiful?" Bori asked. "What, just in this form?"

She shifted, her body bulking up with muscle and fat until she towered over us. The clothing she wore stretched out across her bulk, almost—but not quite—bursting at the seams. I couldn't help but backpedal a bit, though Arnold Wreckt stood there in front of her, his expression serene. "I think that you are beautiful. The two forms, they are just two sides of the same coin, Bori."

He reached out a hand and touched her cheek. "We mean to stop Anton Karmazov, Bori. Will you help us? It will free your sisters, free you, and clear our names. More than that, it will help many people that he would otherwise hurt."

She stepped back from him, her expression impossible to read behind the bulk. She could have swatted him aside, pounded me to jelly, and then scraped up what was left of me to take back to Karmazov. My stomach tensed, and I really wanted to pee as the seconds drew out.

Instead, she twisted her head so her neck popped and then, slowly, she shifted back into her slimmer appearance. "This is stupid. I am stupid." She shook her head, holding her stretched clothing tight around her. "We are all going to die."

"Karmazov can't match Wreckt and you together," I assured her. Each of them had thrown goons around with no issues, and bullets bounced off them. What did we have to fear?

"Do you think he got where he was while being a normal human?" Borislava scoffed at me. "Anton Karmazov is a Talent as well. They used to call him the Cutter, back in the USSR. He worked for the KGB as one of their assassins."

"The Cutter?" I asked.

She shuddered, her arms going tight around herself. "Karmazov the Cutter. In Ukraine, they would send him when factory workers would protest, when work conditions were too awful, too many people were crippled or injured. He would come for the protest leaders, and they would find… *pieces* of them and their families. Everyone would go back to work."

Wreckt stepped forward and hugged her. "He will not do that to us."

I couldn't help but ask, "How does he do it? I mean, I've seen bullets bounce off of Wreckt and you, for that matter."

"I do not know. He does not use it often. Most often, he just uses guns. Once, though, when he was very angry with one of his men, his eyes turned red, and a moment later, the man's body fell apart into pieces."

"What, just…" I frowned.

"As if put through a meat slicer." Borislava shuddered. "The blood came out everywhere, just leaking, his heart was sliced into a dozen pieces, with the rest of him in little cubes, every inch of him, from toes to crown. It was awful. I have had nightmares that he would do it to my sisters and me if we step out of line."

"Okay, so don't get him looking at us funny, got it." I nodded. I wasn't sure why she was so disturbed by it. She had literally pounded *me* into a paste. I had blood coming out of all my orifices at any given point since the start of all this.

I mean, yeah, that had been horrible and painful and awful. I probably needed a few days or hours of downtime to have crying fits about it, but…

I couldn't come up with a 'but.' I probably had gone well past my limit of trauma.

"What about his business deals with the politicians?" I asked, eager to focus on something else, anything else.

She stepped out of Wreckt's arms and looked at me. "If you are serious about taking him down, he keeps extensive details of all his business arrangements. One of my sisters, it is her job to track all of his people and all debts owed and payments made and to record them for him. He keeps his books in his office. If you want evidence of his bribes, those books will give you that."

"So, we nab his books, make sure he doesn't give us the crazy eye, and get your sisters free." I nodded. "This is all doable."

"Is he always like this?" Borislava asked Wreckt.

Wreckt shrugged. "Always."

I ignored the byplay. A plan was starting to come together in my head. It was crazy, it was stupid. It would probably get me killed or chopped up into little meat cubes or arrested.

If it worked, though…

I looked down at the cell phone in my hands, Vasily's phone, and I pulled up the contacts on it.

I began to laugh.

Chapter 14

"Are you certain about this?" Borislava asked for the twentieth or so time since I had explained the plan. Borislava had a van that Karmazov had given her to use, and Wreckt and I were in the back of the van.

We had left Katie's SUV for someone to pick up. I hoped it didn't get stolen with where we had parked it. If it did, I hoped Katie wouldn't hold it against me too much.

"Yeah, this is the best way to do it," I told her. I had sent the details of the plan to Katie, who had texted back that I was an idiot. Between their two votes of confidence, I was really starting to doubt myself. Linus and Lawrence, at least, had thought it was a *great* plan.

"Don't worry, partners," Lawrence said in my ear, "I'm watching, and everything is ready to go. I love this plan."

"Of course he loves it." Wreckt snorted. "If it works, we have millions of people watching, if it doesn't, our deaths will break record numbers of views."

Troublingly, Lawrence didn't argue that point.

We had pulled up in front of Karmazov's club. Apparently, with everything going on, Karmazov had closed it down until things blew over. I was glad of that, because that meant fewer people in the crossfire when things started to happen.

Wreckt reached over and rested a hand on Borislava's shoulder. "We will be fine. This will work."

"I hope so, for all our sakes." Borislava shook her head. "Here we go."

She got out of the van and then came around and opened the back doors. "Out!" she barked. "Both of you, out!"

She gave me a slap as I did so, the blow almost knocking me to my knees. *It's just for the benefit of the thugs watching,* I told myself. Still, she hadn't needed to hit me *that* hard.

With Arnold and I out of the van, she pushed us both along toward the doors to the club. "Tell Sergei and Karmazov that I got them both!"

Maybe I was just nervous, but it felt like there were a *lot* of goons out there.

I had the phone and camera rolling and the earbud in my ear. I hoped the live stream audience appreciated the risks I was taking for their entertainment.

As we came up to the doors, Sergei appeared, his spider tattoo looking as if it were about to crawl into his mouth. "How did you get them?"

"I pretended to work out a deal, and they agreed to come in to talk," Borislava sneered. "They fell for my story, now they are here. Are we going to do this out here in the street or inside?"

Sergei scowled at her, but he stepped out of the way, and two of his goons opened the doors.

Borislava pushed us through the doors, shoving me hard enough that I stumbled and nearly fell. I shot her a glare; there was playing it up, and there was too much.

"The little guy has nothing to say, now, eh?" Sergei laughed at me.

I had plenty to say, but I was saving it for when it mattered. I kept my mouth shut.

We got into the main dance floor of the club, and Anton Karmazov came down the steps from his office. Apparently, the labor shortage had hit even the criminal element; he hadn't had anyone in yet to repair the broken office windows or the smashed skylight from where Wreckt had thrown a few of his thugs through. *What a shame,* I thought to myself.

The bar was the same, at least, running the length of the room, with an exit door near the back that probably led to the same alleyway that Arnold and I had escaped through the last time we had been here. I couldn't help but notice that, with the lights up and no music and flashing lights to distract, the place had a cheap, tawdry look, like a movie set that was seen from the wrong angle.

"I brought them," Borislava called out to him. "As I promised. Will you set my sisters free?"

Anton looked at her, then at the pair of us. He waved at Sergei. "Bring her sisters."

"But, Boss…" Sergei started to say.

Karmazov just looked at him. Sergei nodded quickly and rushed into the back with several goons in tow.

There were about twenty or thirty of his guys in here, all of them armed. I panned the camera around, taking it in. "So… uh, nice place you got here."

"Now he talks," Karmazov hissed. "I wanted to be sure it was you. Some people seem to think you are someone else. That you were *replaced* by someone else."

"Nope, one hundred percent me, Eddie Connors, the best actor's agent anywhere," I told him. "You can check out my website, it's at E dot C dot—"

"Take his phone, check them both for wires," Karmazov interrupted me.

Several goons stepped forward. Before I could say or do anything, they took my phone and smashed it to bits. They didn't see or didn't bother with the earbuds, but they frisked Wreckt and I very thoroughly. *Very* thoroughly.

"Hey," I squawked, "that's all me down there. *Careful* with that, I need it for later."

"They are clean," one of the goons reported as they stepped back.

Karmazov came closer. I didn't miss how he stayed well out of reach of Wreckt. He also didn't get too close to Borislava, which told me he didn't trust her. *That's unfortunate. It would be nice if one of them could smash him to a pulp.*

"I shot you in head before. That normally does the trick, but not you," Karmazov said in a hard voice as he stared at me. "You have a Talent, some kind of healing?"

"I'm BENT, maybe a Talent, who knows?" I smiled. "Look, we got off on the wrong foot. Arnold and I never wanted to get into it with your guys. Some things happened, blows were exchanged. We were just defending ourselves, you understand, right?"

"I will experiment on you, see what kind of damage you can take." Karmazov ignored my words. "Over and over again, until you beg me for death."

"I would really rather that we talked all this out." I gestured between us. "Have you read *The Art of Compromise*? Fantastic book, I think there's a way for both of us to get what we want—"

"Silence!" Karmazov bellowed, his voice echoing around the big empty space in a terrifying fashion.

He turned and looked at Wreckt. "You, I could have used you as a foot soldier when I first started building my empire. Why do you follow this imbecile?"

"He is my friend," Wreckt told him.

"You killed too many of my men to let you live. I think we will see how indestructible you are…"

Sergei came back into the main room. He had two women with him. I assumed they were

Borislava's sisters. Karmazov stepped back from us and looked at Borislava. "Here we are. As I said, your sisters, delivered, alive and well. Here is the proof that I have not harmed them."

Borislava hurried over and embraced her two sisters, and they started crying and talking in what I assumed was Ukrainian.

"A happy reunion." Karmazov smiled. His smile vanished a moment later. "The three of you have become an irritation. I have given you many things. I have brought you to this land of plenty, I have provided for you, always there is more that you want. You want freedom, you want out…"

He snapped his fingers, and several of his goons moved over, pulling Borislava's sisters back from her. "I am tired of it. You brought them because you wanted them and you free? You should have done it from loyalty. The fact that you asked for more proves that you will never be loyal. I need loyal foot troops. Instead, I will use you as an example, to your sisters, of the cost of not being completely loyal to me."

Borislava's expression and posture shifted. I could tell she was about to go into combat mode.

He snapped his fingers at her. "If you try to change into your monster form, I will have them killed." His men brought up weapons and aimed at her two sisters, and the fight went out of Borislava.

Oh, crap, I didn't plan on this, I thought. For him to keep the three of them, sure, I expected that. For him to kill Borislava to make an example out of her? That was all new levels of messed up.

"Look, uh, Mister Karmazov, I think maybe you're going off the deep end, here," I spoke up, aware that Wreckt had gone tense next to me. I didn't want him going off, not when they held all the cards. That would get all of us dead.

I spoke quickly, trying to get his attention, trying to keep him from giving the order to kill Borislava or her sisters, "I mean, how you run your business is none of mine, I suppose, but killing the person who brought us in seems a little backward. Like, rewards and bonuses, a fat separation bonus… that kind of thing seems like a better arrangement."

Karmazov turned toward me, his eyes flashing with anger. No, not flashing, *flaring*, like, red. "How stupid are you? Do you have any idea how much pain I will cause you and your friend? You would be smart to beg for a quick death. Instead, you continue to insolently mouth off."

A goon rushed over. "Boss, there's a problem out front…"

"I told you, he told *me* he wanted to see us," a loud voice shouted. "Out of my way, you idiots."

The governor came through the doors. Following him came the Chicago mayor.

They paused as they saw Wreckt and I, then the governor blinked. "So, uh, you got him? That's a relief. Is that why you wanted to see us, so we can call off the manhunt?"

"I didn't want to see either of you," Karmazov hissed. "Why are you here?"

"You sent us both messages." The governor looked over at the mayor, who gave him a head bob of agreement. "We got them on our personal cell phones."

"I didn't send you any messages," Karmazov growled. "The last place that either of you two should be is here, especially with all the media attention on the both of you."

"Yeah, uh, so this is probably my fault, again." I raised a hand. "You see, that cell phone your goons smashed used to be that guy, Vasily's, you know, the one that Arnold threw through your window up there after you shot me?" I pointed at the office window and then the skylight.

I went on, "Anyway, I figured the best way to work through all of this was to get us all here in person, talk through everything and—"

Karmazov spun to face me, his eyes glowing red. I stopped talking. Not because I wanted to, mind, but because nothing in my throat and mouth wanted to respond. I tasted blood and coughed a spurt of it, and blood and pieces of my tongue fell out of my mouth. I stared down at it in shock, horror, and fascination. There wasn't any pain. Not at first. Those cuts had severed the nerves; I didn't feel anything.

That was, until it all started knitting itself together in my mouth and throat. *That* hurt. A lot. I gritted my teeth, not wanting to choke on my own blood if I screamed from the pain.

Anton Karmazov came over, his eyes glowing red. "I can cut you into tiny pieces, little boy."

"If you hurt him again, you'll get Wreckt," Arnold said in an ominous tone.

"I don't care how strong you are." Karmazov glared at him. "I will cut you into tiny pieces and flush you down my toilets."

"Not the toilets again, boss," Sergei protested. "Last time, they kept clogging for weeks."

Karmazov spun on him, and Sergei flinched back.

My mouth had knitted back together, and I rotated my jaw. "Okay, that's a pretty neat trick, what is it, you shoot invisible laser beams or something? I mean, you didn't even cut up the outside of my mouth, just the inside…"

Karmazov spun back.

I didn't feel it, again, but the inside of my mouth filled with hot blood once more, and blood dribbled down the corners of my mouth.

The governor started to hurl. "Oh, that's so gross. Can you please not do that in front of us?"

Chicago's mayor looked on with fascination, "No, no, don't stop on my account. Can you do that anywhere? Can you hit him in the groin?"

Around the agony of my mouth knitting itself together, I noticed a vein pulsing at Karmazov's temple. He spun on the two politicians. "I pay you two idiots to keep things quiet. Now you have held press conferences, they have mentioned my name on the news. My *name*."

"It's not a big deal, you got them both, I'm sure we can make this all go away," the governor assured him.

"Yeah, for enough money, I'll make anything go away." The mayor nodded, her goblin-face still intently focused on me. "You could shoot both these boys in broad daylight downtown, and I'll tell the District Attorney and the police to look the other way."

The governor nodded his head quickly. "We've kept your purchases of property quiet. We've kept the police and investigators out of it."

"Shut *up*," Karmazov bit out.

"I mean, they're only telling it like it is." I coughed a little bit, my throat and mouth still hurting as I talked. I wanted them talking, though, and if these two idiots pissed off Karmazov, maybe I would get lucky, and they would have a complete falling out.

The Russian mobster turned to face me, and this time, his expression was so far gone to rage that I took a step back and closed my mouth. Wreckt started to step in front of me, and I reached out a hand to stop him.

Karmazov spun back to the two politicians. "I want you both out of here. This was arrangement, I tell you what to do, and you do it. You do not come to meet me unless *I* tell you to do it. You do not argue, you do not ask questions." He snapped his fingers at the mayor, who was still staring intently at me, and her eyes went to him. "Do you understand?"

"Yes." She looked a bit disappointed that he hadn't zapped me with his laser eyes a third time.

"Of course." The governor nodded quickly.

"Now, who all is here? Who knows that you came?" Karmazov asked.

"Well my state trooper escort, and her police escort," the governor began.

"Then go to them and get out of here. Do not come back unless *I* tell you to come," Karmazov snarled. The pair of crooked politicians backed away from him. If it hadn't been for the pain I was in and the fact that this guy planned on killing us as soon as the two of them left, I might have felt gratified by the fear in their eyes.

"I think they get it. Unfortunately, they can't leave just yet," a voice spoke as the doors opened and a swarm of men in black body armor came through. They had their weapons slung, though as Anton Karmazov's men brought their weapons around, their weapons came up. They had a huge variety of weapons, too. I saw what looked like machine guns, some more net guns, what looked like a rocket launcher, and even a trio of flamethrowers.

At their front was a big man. "Anton Karmazov, stop right there."

Quite suddenly, there were a lot of guns aimed in all different directions. I might have felt better, except I had the feeling that our surprise guests were not going to be helping us out.

Chapter 15

These guys looked a whole lot like the black ops goons that had attacked us the previous night. In fact, the guy at the lead had the same handsome face and confident voice as the leader from the night before, which didn't make a lot of sense, seeing as I'd seen Borislava turn him to mush.

With how casually he and his team had walked in here, I felt a whole lot of concern about how badly my plan had gone awry.

"Who the hell are you?" Karmazov spun to the intruders. I wanted the answer to that myself.

"My name doesn't matter. I'm with an agency that has an interest in your prisoners," the man answered.

"FBI?" Karmazov demanded. "I have arrangements with them."

"After your goons had their little run in with the local FBI team, they're not particularly happy with you, Mister Karmazov." The man smirked as he said that. "My organization, though, can smooth things over. You pay your taxes, you pay off the right politicians, and you feed the FBI information on Talents like Borislava over there on a regular basis so they're liable to get back on board, even if your people did damage a few of theirs."

He flashed a humorless smile. "My organization, though, we broker in knowledge. Mister Connors, there, may know the location of someone we are after. Even if he doesn't, his regenerative abilities are quite interesting. We'd like to take him apart and see how it works."

"I can do that myself," Karmazov hissed. "Get out of my club."

"You don't get to tell me what to do," the leader of the black ops team told him. "I know how your little trick with the eyes works, too. Sure, you can take out one or two of us, maybe even me, but it only works if you have a chance to really look at someone and manifest those little force fields inside the target. It won't work so well when the chopper overhead puts a hellfire shredder missile into you."

Even as he spoke, I heard the *thud-thud-thud* of a helicopter banking overhead.

"So, here's what's going to happen," the black ops leader went on. "You are going to give me Mister Connors, and we all part ways. I'll take him back to an off-books site where we take him apart piece by piece to find out everything we can about him. You can keep Arnold Wreckt, he's the one that killed your men. You can make your example out of Miss Borislava there. We don't care about either of them, bruisers are a dime a dozen."

I couldn't help a little snort. "He just said you're going to get Wreckt.'"

That startled a laugh out of a couple of Karmazov's goons. He glared at them and then back at me, and I shut my mouth.

"The little man there is the annoying one. I really wanted to kill him myself." Karmazov's tone turned petulant.

"If it makes you feel better, having run his psychological profile, it will probably hurt him worse to kill his friends. He's wired that way," the black ops team leader told him.

Who the hell is this guy, how does he have a profile on me, who does he work for, and how is he still alive after I saw Borislava bounce him face first off an I-beam?

"Uh, hey, do I get a vote in this?" I raised a hand.

"Shut up," they both answered.

"No, really." Seeing as things couldn't get much worse and that they had both sort of spilled all their secrets, I didn't see any reason to shut up at this point. "You see, there's something I want you all to know, before your guys disappear me and do horrible things to me, and before Anton Karmazov kills my friends in a horrible fashion, and before the governor and mayor both slip away to their police escorts."

The two politicians, who had been inching toward the door, froze. The governor looked around guiltily, and the mayor flipped me the bird.

"What is it you want to say, little boy?" Karmazov demanded. "What do you think will make any difference at this point? Or do you wish to waste our time with further insolence?"

"You know, I was total shit with that camera phone." I pointed at the debris of Vasily's cell phone. "I mean, *really* bad. Even with artificial stabilization and a lot of help from the software, half the time I had the camera in the wrong direction to get any shot of what was going on. Thankfully, our viewers only had to rely on that a little bit."

"What is your point?" Karmazov scowled at me, his eyes flashing red. I figured he was just about ready to zap my whole head and see if my brain could knit itself back together from it.

The black ops guy's eyes widened, though, and I could see his eyes going upward toward the ceiling.

"Oh, I just wanted to tell you that I've got a really good camera guy. He uses these drones in a whole network, and they're getting great footage of all this." I smiled.

"We just hit a million viewers," Lawrence spoke in my earbud, which he had linked to his drones. The drones that he had flown in the broken skylight while Anton Karmazov and all his men were focused on Wreckt and me. "We have thirty or so mega-chats, too, but you can thank them all later."

"Oh, hey, I think we just got a record for most number of live viewers," I told them. "So please, say hello to all your viewers, guys. Special thanks to the mega-chats, I'll thank you all when I get time!"

Everything went crazy at that point. The governor and mayor both sprinted for the door. Borislava shifted as Karmazov's men were distracted, and she dove into the ones with guns on her sisters.

Wreckt drove forward as well, bellowing as he laid into the thugs between him and Karmazov. I did the smart thing and scarpered for cover.

Guns started firing in all directions. Faster than I thought possible, black ops guys and Russians were shooting at each other and at us. I felt a bullet tear through my shoulder as I rushed forward, catching Borislava's sisters, one by each arm, and pulling them with me behind the cover of the bar. As I had seen earlier, there was a door there, and I pushed them both toward it. "Go, there's two guys, Clarence and Trev, they'll be waiting for you outside the back door!"

The two women stayed low and ran that way, and I was tempted to run right after them. The problem was, I couldn't leave my friends behind.

I popped my head up and took a look.

A black ops goon went flying just over my head to slam into liquor bottles. "Sorry, the bar is closed!" Wreckt called out.

The goon groaned and rolled off to thud onto the floor next to me.

I laughed to myself. "Wreckt 'em… darn near killed him."

I ignored Wreckt's advice, looking around for one person who I knew would be here somewhere. I knew because I had told her I didn't want her anywhere near this mess, so of course, she would have ignored what I told her to do and come anyway.

I didn't see Katie, though I did see a gout of flame from one of the black ops goons come my way. It hit the broken bottles of liquor behind me, and then other bottles began to explode into flame as the heat caused the glass to shatter. I dropped down out of sight, no longer in safety as the entire bar area started to go up. "Fire, why did it have to be fire?"

The black ops goon next to me started to scream as the liquor covering him ignited. I knew exactly how that felt. I fled the fire, running right into the middle of the carnage.

Borislava had caught Sergei by the ankle and was swinging him around like a pissed off *abuela* using her sandal to discipline unruly children. Men scattered away from her, some of them with enough clarity of mind to shoot at her. I wasn't too sure if she would recognize friend from foe, so I got the hell out of her way as well. That put me shoulder to shoulder with a black ops goon, who, on realizing that, brought his shotgun around toward my face. I flinched back and down, and as I did so, he froze, then his head fell off his neck into many small pieces.

Karmazov stood behind him, his expression focused and his eyes glowing red.

He swung that gaze around, and three more black ops guys fell. As he looked at Arnold Wreckt's back, though, I dove forward and tackled him to the ground.

There was a roar and a howl, and something screamed through the space we had both occupied. Something hot and wet splashed over me, and I looked back to see that three of Karmazov's men had basically exploded, and this horrible-looking combination of lawnmower blades and missile had smashed into the ground beyond them. It skidded at least twenty feet before it slammed into the burning bar.

"Oooh," Lawrence called out in my ear, "so *that's* what a hellfire shredder missile looks like. Wow, I've got that from like three angles. Perfect timing, too. Going to replay that one in slow motion…"

Karmazov elbowed me in the face, and I fell back from where I'd had him down on the ground. He sat up, looking at me, then at his men who had been shredded where he had been standing. For just a second, I thought he might even thank me for saving his life. Then his eyes flashed red.

"Shit." I dove to the side, sliding across the floor between shouting and screaming men. Next to me, one guy's knee exploded into thinly sliced chunks of meat and bone, followed immediately by spurting blood. "Sorry about using you for cover," I told him as he fell in front of me, screaming. His face fell apart right after that, though, so I wasn't sure if he had heard me.

Someone caught me by the shoulder and pulled me to my feet, firing in the direction of Karmazov. I was going to thank him, until I recognized the black ops team leader. He spoke while he fired, "You're remarkably slippery, Connors."

He drew out what looked like a pair of manacles, but before he could force them on me, Wreckt caught *him* by the shoulder and pulled him away.

To give him credit, he stayed calm as Wreckt pulled him away, transitioning to his pistol and firing point-blank into Wreckt's face, and as bullets bounced off my friend's eyeballs, he shifted over to an electric goad, which he jammed into Wreckt's hand, just by the wrist where Wreckt was holding him.

My friend let him go, and the guy dodged back out of reach and vanished into the chaos.

"Are you alright?" Wreckt shrugged off a rain of bullets from one of the Russians standing next to him and drove an elbow into the man's sternum. The goon went spinning end over end and smashed into the flaming bar, vanishing with a scream.

"Of course, I'm great, couldn't be better…"

"Oh, crap." I caught a flash of glowing red from the side and jumped forward, putting myself between Karmazov and Wreckt.

I didn't feel anything, and at first, I thought I was fine, right up until a football-sized chunk of my chest started to fall out of me along with way too much blood. *Force fields, huh, that's pretty cool,* I thought, *what a world we live in…*

Then the pain hit me as my nerves and tissue started to regrow. I dropped, unable to stand. Over my shoulder, I saw Wreckt throw one of the Russian thugs at Karmazov, then I ended up face-down on the ground, screaming, as my chest knit itself back together.

Someone caught me by the foot and started dragging me across the floor. My first thought was that I was being pulled to safety. As my face dragged across the concrete, though, I started to wonder if I was wrong.

I rolled over, getting a look back, and recognized the black ops team leader, who had caught me by the foot. "You are persistent." I kicked at him with my other foot, trying to get him to let me go.

"Got to keep my eye on the prize." His voice was calm as he blocked my kick. A Russian mobster came at him from the side, and he fired his pistol with his off-hand, not even looking as the foe toppled.

"That was a nice move. You could really make a bundle in Hollywood as a stuntman or combat choreographer!" I called to him as I caught on to a structural beam and tried to kick my foot free of his grasp.

"I love what I do, thanks," he said as he jabbed me with his electric goad. My whole body tensed up, and he yanked me free and kept dragging me toward the doors.

A flying Russian caught him from the side, though, and that loosened his grip enough for me to wiggle free and run back toward the chaos. *Why am I going this way?* I asked myself, even as I ran into a brawling group of black ops guys and Russian thugs. Punches, kicks, baton blows, and knives jabbed out at one another, all from so close that I didn't know how they even knew who they were hitting. As I caught a baton blow to the side of the head, I dropped to my knees, catching a kick to my ribs that sent me rolling along the ground.

I looked up in time to see Bori plow into the whole group of them, Wreckt not far behind her. "Now, good job, keep a low center of gravity, yeah, like that, good!" Wreckt told her.

She let out a bellow and lifted the whole group of them off the ground, her arms straining.

"Good, keep the weight centered over your hips, use those hip muscles and glutes. Very good," Wreckt shouted to her.

He had a thug in each hand and one of them was kicking him in the face, though my friend seemed oblivious to the blows as he watched his girlfriend.

Borislava let out a grunt of effort and threw the group of men against the wall, most of them going limp from the impact, though a few of them started crawling away.

"We're cleaning up," I couldn't help but call out.

Just as I said that, a fist caught hold of my hair and pulled me painfully to my feet. "That's just about enough of that." I recognized the team leader's voice, even as he brought up a big knife to hold it against my throat. "Not another move,

Wreckt, or we'll see if your little buddy can regenerate from complete decapitation."

"You can do that with a knife?" I asked in surprise. "I thought you needed like a sword or something."

"It's all in the wrist," my captor told me with a smirk. He started backing us toward the door again.

Karmazov came from around the bar, his eyes blazing with red energy. "You come into my territory, you wreck my club? Do you really think that I care what you do to that little weasel?"

"No, but they might," my captor nodded at Wreckt and Borislava.

"He's all yours," Wreckt told her.

When he was younger, Anton Karmazov might have turned in time to take her down. He was too slow, though, as she covered the distance between them, planting a kick to his sternum that made my whole body shudder. The Russian mob boss went flying to slap wetly against the back wall of his club, and his remains hung there, just below the shattered windows from his office.

"Nice kick," Wreckt told her.

"Thank you, I played football as a child." She nodded.

"That seems to have settled Mister Karmazov," my captor said in a cold voice. "I don't see any of his men left in a fighting state."

I didn't see much of anyone left. The flames from the bar had begun to spread to the rest of the building. Pretty soon it would all be engulfed. I wondered if we had enough evidence to clear our names. I wondered if my captor even cared that we had aired his dirty laundry.

"You can't escape," Wreckt told him. "I will chase you down."

"Not if you're trying to take care of your injured girlfriend," The black ops team lead answered. "Hit her."

I realized he was talking on his radio and who he was talking to at the same time.

Overhead, I heard the chopper and, even as I started to shout a warning, another hellfire shredder round screamed in through the roof and smashed into Borislava. Fire and pieces of missile exploded in all directions, and the impact sent her bouncing toward the back of the club.

"Huh, I didn't figure that would work, but good to know it can at least knock her off her feet," my captor noted. As Wreckt turned to check on

Borislava, the black ops guy dragged me the other direction by my hair.

"Why are you doing this?" I demanded. "How are you even still alive?"

"I'm like the fucking energizer bunny, kid. I keep coming back over and over."

"That's like Jason, or that other horror movie guy," I felt the need to point out. "The bunny just keeps going and going and…"

"Enough," my captor snapped. "I am doing this because if you know even a scrap of information on Lloyd, all this is worth it. And I was telling the truth when I said we wanted to see how your regeneration worked. I have to wonder, is it a gland? Some kind of cellular or even molecular thing? Imagine if we could have an army like you, who could shrug off otherwise lethal hits. I have a special interest in it myself, so I'll be very thorough."

"No one has ever figured out how to give Talents to anyone," I protested.

"How will we know what's possible without trying?" My captor laughed. "And really, I enjoy the process, if not the results."

We were almost to the doors. I knew that once he had me outside, he would have reinforcements and support, and Wreckt would never find me.

He looked over his shoulder, and I followed his gaze. One of his remaining people, one of the ones armed with a flamethrower, had stepped into the doorway, presumably to provide cover for his retreat.

As we both watched, she pulled off the black helmet and mask.

My eyes widened as I recognized Katie.

"Let go of my boyfriend, you son of a bitch." She fired the flamethrower right at us.

Chapter 16

As the heat washed down on us, my captor finally flinched. His hold on me loosened, and I tore myself away, leaving him with a handful of hair and not much else.

I instinctively recoiled from the heat and flame, rushing backward from it, even as the black ops team leader went the other way. Katie whipped the flamethrower to create a wall of fire between me and him.

At least some of the stuff got him, and his arm was on fire as he backed away.

I had seen how fast he could move, though, and I tried to shout a warning to Katie.

I was too late. He brought his pistol up, firing twice into her.

Wreckt came out of nowhere, then, catching his firing hand and clenching his fist down on the pistol and hand together.

I could hear the goon's fingers break and the pistol metal snap at the same time. My eyes, though, had gone to Katie, who had crumpled to the ground. I rushed toward her, heedless of the spreading flames, and caught her up.

"Oh, shit," I said, feeling at her stomach and chest and finding hot, spreading blood.

"Now *that's* what that feels like." Katie coughed. "I've never been shot before. I mean, in movies, sure, but not in real life."

I couldn't staunch the blood flow. I didn't know first aid; I had never had to patch anyone up before. There was a lot of it. I knew enough to know that was bad.

I looked up at Wreckt, my eyes hot with anger. He still held the black ops team leader, and he raised an eyebrow. I shook my head.

"You wanted Connors, but instead, you got Wreckt." Arnold swung the man into a metal support column and then let what remained of him fall to the floor. Wreckt rushed over to me.

"We need to get her out of here, to a hospital." I had her blood all over my hands from trying to staunch the flow.

"No…" Katie protested. "You can't do anything. Just get out."

"I'm not leaving you." I reached under her, lifting her in my arms. Wreckt tried to help me, but I caught her up on my own. She seemed so light, and I found myself sobbing as I hurried along with her, dodging falling bits of debris as Karmazov's club began to fall apart. Fear drove me faster as I rushed to the back door. Fear of the flame was a physical thing, a thing that drove panic into my brain. Worse, though, was the fear of loss, the fear that I was going to lose Katie.

We got out the back. Borislava was there in the alleyway, reunited with her sisters. Clarence and Trevor had the cars waiting there as well. "We need to get her to the hospital," I started. "Bring up the SUV, lower the back seats. We can lay her flat and—"

"Not going to work," Katie mumbled.

I looked down at her, and she had gone so pale and still that for a second, I thought she had died.

I lowered her to the ground, panic making my hands tremble as I brushed her hair out of her face. "Katie, Katie, are you with me still?"

"Always," she told me in a weak voice.

"You better stay with me," I gasped at her. "I love you."

"Good to hear," Katie answered. "I love you… too."

"Alright, they're pulling the car up. We'll get you in it and to a hospital and—"

"Not going to work. I'm dying." She gazed at me. "Believe me, Eddie, I've been close enough to it before to know." She gave a weak gasp. "I guess my story ends… here, my love."

She went still. It was such a certain stillness that I knew that her heart had stopped, that her breathing had stopped.

I felt desperation claw through me. "How far to a hospital?" I demanded.

Clarence answered, "Fifteen minutes, man."

She didn't have fifteen minutes. She didn't have even one minute. Her heart had stopped, her blood had pumped out, her body was in shock…

Her body… her Talent…

My head snapped up, my gaze going to the burning building that we had all escaped. "Wreckt"—I looked over at my friend—"she's a phoenix, right?"

"Eddie…" Wreckt's eyebrows lowered in concern.

"Fire regenerates her," I told him.

"From age, Eddie," Wreckt told me. "This is something else. Besides… she's already dead."

"No!" I snapped. I bent down and picked her up.

Wreckt got in front of me. "Eddie, if it has to be done, let me do it. I am nearly indestructible."

"Nearly doesn't mean all the way. Fire still can burn you," I told him.

"Fire *will* burn you, and if it burns you up all the way, there won't be anything to regenerate," Wreckt told me. "Don't do this."

"I don't have a choice," I told him. "I would rather die with her than live without. Now, I love you like a brother, but get the *hell* out of my way."

He moved. I stumbled forward. Fear ate at me. I hated fire. With every step forward, my body and brain screamed at me to turn around and run. I thought back to that horrid moment that the fire had burned into me as a teenager, where it had ruptured my eyeballs and burned my flesh down to a horrid, crispy nightmare.

I fought to take each step, my breath coming in ragged pants, my face drawn back in a rictus of pain and fear.

I made it to the door, somehow. On the edge of it, in the heat of the blaze that had engulfed the former Russian mob boss's club, I looked back at my friends. Clarence and Trev both looking on in fear and wonder. Borislava standing with her sisters. And of course, Arnold Wreckt staring at me with stern attention. He gave me a last nod, a final salute. That gave me the resolution I needed to turn back to the blaze.

I stepped into the fire. I could feel it engulf me, singeing away my clothing, my eyebrows, and my stupid hair. It ate into my flesh, melting my skin and tissue. I couldn't scream, I couldn't breathe, agony washed over me as I strode forward, every bit of me burning up, burning up faster than my body could heal itself.

In my arms, Katie's body seemed to grow lighter and lighter. As I fell to my knees, I could feel her rise out of my arms, lifted by the heat of the terrible flame, even as it consumed me.

For one wonderful moment, she stood above me, whole and entire in the flame, a presence that I sensed, for I could no longer see.

Then I collapsed, and my world vanished.

Chapter 17

Katie strode out of the inferno alone. The fire danced her dark hair, like a lover's caress. Her green eyes were alight with it, glowing and reflecting the flame. As she came to the ruined doorway, she looked back at the flames, a single golden tear falling from her eyes. Then she turned away from the fire and walked to join her friends.

It was a singular perfect moment that struck me to the core.

Then the credits began to roll.

"I can't believe they killed me," I grumbled to her.

"Shut up." Katie snuggled against me in the reclining theater seats. "The story works better this way, far more tragic." We had lifted the armrest between us and spent the whole movie like this. It was great.

Not that I was going to let that distract me from my complaints.

"I *died*." I waved at the screen.

"The *character* died." Katie rolled her eyes. "The director made the decision to kill your *character*. It was purely based off audience feedback."

I held up my hands. "*And* they recast me. I can't believe that you and Arnold and even Borislava got to play themselves, even C-dawg and Trev!"

"You were the agent for all of them except for me." Katie pointed out. "You negotiated their contracts, and you got them the roles."

I ignored her entirely logical arguments and went on, "And Linus cast that Radbluff guy from the Horry Cobbler movies to play me. He doesn't even look like me, and he's, like, thirty years old."

"He did a fantastic job with the material, you have to admit," Katie assured me.

"He got to kiss you on screen," I grumbled. That was the real thing that had bothered me, I could admit.

"You get to kiss me and do a lot more in real life, are you *really* complaining about that?" Katie arched an eyebrow at me.

I shut up.

We stood up and joined the others headed for the doors. On the way, we passed a movie poster for Clarence's period drama. It had Borislava and Wreckt on the front, as the queen and her duke. I couldn't help a smirk as I saw that. Wreckt had really shown his acting chops and Borislava, for her measure, wasn't a slouch. It had already been snubbed, hard, by the Oscars, but we had stacked up a ton of awards overseas. Even the dubbed versions were making a killing. Clarence had even had an offer from Bollywood to make a musical action number out of his script, and they wanted some of the original cast.

They were going to need a stand-in for Arnold Wreckt, though. I had heard him sing in the shower before; he couldn't carry a tune in a bucket.

We met the others outside. Our group had caught a late-night showing—it was the only showing we could get tickets for, as the movie theater had been sold out otherwise. Market projections showed that *Get Wreckt* was going to still lose money, due to the costs of special effects, actor pay, script writing, and advertising. That's what Linus told me, anyway, which worked fine for me since my actors had gotten paid, which meant I had gotten paid.

Somehow, despite all of us losing money, Katie had replaced the two cars she had lost, Arnold had replaced all of his gym equipment we'd had to leave behind at our old apartment, and Borislava and her sisters had gotten new apartments and expensive immigration lawyers.

I had my doubts about his politics, but I couldn't argue with Norm Linus's business sense.

"So, what next?" I asked them. One more reason for the night showing had been to avoid too many people recognizing us. Between the live stream and the two movies, Wreckt had become a sensation overnight.

Plus, there was the whole concern about some secretive organization that might still want to kidnap and experiment on me. I hoped that was behind me, though.

Clarence looked nervous. "I was going to work the next script. Linus told me he thinks it's a sure thing, but he wants me to do some research."

"Okay, that sounds good." I looked at the others.

Wreckt and Borislava stood close together, touching and more than just touching. There was a… *comfort* that I saw and recognized between the two of them. A level of trust between them that at another time I might have envied.

Instead, my hand reached out and caught Katie's. She gave my hand a little squeeze.

"Well"—I looked around at them—"Clarence needs some research for his next movie. Where's it set?"

"The border area of Texas. It's going to be another period drama, the Mexican-American War, set against the fall of the Alamo," Clarence told us. "I want to show the struggle for freedom as a contrast against the traditions of a different society. Also, there's going to be a brothel and a lot of topless honeys."

I rolled my eyes at that, but Katie just laughed. You could take the gangster out of the hood, but you couldn't take the hood out of the gangster, I guess.

"Huh." I frowned. I looked at Wreckt. "You still want to help people?"

He gave me a broad smile. "Of course."

"I hear there's a cartel problem down that way," I mused. "Might be a good angle to look at making another action movie."

Katie laughed, "Get Wreckt Two? Getting Wreckt-er?"

"I was thinking maybe Wreckt and Connor?" I raised an eyebrow.

She snorted. "Leave the naming things to someone with real talent, okay, Eddie?"

I laughed. "Okay, sure. So… you guys in?"

Wreckt smiled. "Journey to Texas, fighting some cartel thugs, it sounds like a fun time."

"Maybe I'll get a cowboy hat," I joked.

We laughed. It was a good time. We were on top of the world. I knew it couldn't last. I knew that if I kept walking into the fire, one day, I wouldn't walk out of it.

That was fine, because I had people to walk into that fire with me.

The End

We hope that you enjoyed this title and look forward to many more to come. Please, leave us a review! Reviews matter to all of our authors.

And don't forget to check out the latest edition of **Car Wars**

http://www.sjgames.com/car-wars/

Or the other amazing titles from Steve Jackson Games

http://www.sjgames.com

…or the latest in the Car Warriors: Autoduel Chronicle fiction series.
https://threeravenspublishing.com/car-warriors-autoduel-chronicles/

Take a look at some of our other award-winning series at
https://threeravenspublishing.com/series-universes/

Visit us at
https://www.threeravenspublishing.com and sign up for our newsletter for the latest and greatest news on upcoming titles and events.

Other series and titles you might enjoy.

ROBERT SILVERBERG
HAWKSBILL
TIMES TWO

DECLAN FINN
Demons Forever
Honor at Stake
Live and Let Bite
Good to the Last Drop
The Dragon Award Nominated Series
FREE on Kindle Unlimited!

AVAILABLE ON
AMAZON
JOINT TASK FORCE
13
HOLDING THE LINE
BETWEEN HEAVEN AND HELL

MYSTERY,
MAGIC &
MAYHEM
WITH A TWIST
OF ROMANCE
J.F. POSTHUMUS
ON AMAZON
FIND ME

B.E.N.T.
BIOLOGIC   ENHANCED   NASCENT   TALENT

THE RAVEN
AND
THE CROW
MICHAEL K. FALGIANI
FIND ME
ON AMAZON

STARFLIGHT

IT CAME FROM THE
TRAILER PARK

You can also keep up to date with our latest release announcements on Scifi.radio and get some of the best fandom programing on the planet.

Scifi for your Wifi

And don't forget to check out our other Sponsors and Affiliates

A southern Appalachian jewel for craft beer lovers, Buck Bald Brewing offers something for everyone. With delicious, locally brewed beverages from across the spectrum, Buck Bald Brewing offers craft brews that are consistently amazing.

From the dark and smooth Shesquatch Scottish ale, to the intense hops of

Hippibilly IPA, to the puckering sour of the blackberry and cinnamon in Berry My Heart at the Trailer Park, and more than 60+ rotating brews, you'll find what you're looking for and more.

With smiling faces behind the bar ready to help you find your next favorite brew, a constantly rotating selection of delicious craft beverages, toe-tapping tunes always playing, and the biggest games on TV, you can kick your feet up in either Copperhill, Tennessee or Murphy, North Carolina and immerse yourself in the Buck Bald Brewing experience. So, come out, fill a pint, fill a growler, and fill your mind at your new favorite family-owned craft brewery.

To discover more visit us at buckbaldbrewing.com or follow us on Facebook @buckbaldbrewing and @buckbaldbrewingmurphy.

Vesper Wren's
TRAILER PARK
PIXIE
PUNCH
• A PEACH STRAWBERRY SELTZER •
BUCK BALD BREWING

BRAXTON
HICKS
MIDNIGHT MOCHA MILK
STOUT
BUCK BALD BREWING

www.ingramcontent.com/pod-product-compliance
Lightning Source LLC
Chambersburg PA
CBHW020748310726
48969CB00002B/470